pardon's
PRICE

Diane Yoder

Ridgeway Publishing
Medina, NY 14103

PARDON'S PRICE

*To order additional copies,
please visit your local
bookstore or contact*

**Ridgeway Publishing
3161 Fruit Avenue
Medina, NY 14103
USA
ph: (888) 822-7894
fax: (585) 798-9016**

Cover design by Rosetta Mullet

ISBN: 978-09848888-0-1

Printed in the United States of America

DEDICATION

This book is dedicated first to my Lord, who has richly blessed me with a heritage that makes life worth living. He deserves all my praise.

I also dedicate this book to my parents, who chose to take me into their home many years ago and to call me their own. *Pardon's Price* is born out of the legacy of this special kind of love. I appreciate what you stand for, Dad and Mom, and I love you both.

ACKNOWLEDGMENTS

I want to thank God for the privilege He has granted in allowing my dream of a lifetime to come true. This book is primarily *His* story.

A special thanks to my editors and publisher for the many hours you put into this project. My aspirations were made possible through you.

Also, a special thanks to my family and friends for believing in me and my ability to write. You played an important part in the shaping of my dream.

PROLOGUE

He could see them now, the tall buildings rising toward the sky in the distance, looming like great, hulking shapes in the darkness of the night. Justin Gallus straightened in the saddle, his weariness dissolving at the sight. Home was inside that great city of Rome—home, and rest for his aching body. He had been traveling for nearly half a day, leading a group of tired soldiers from the battleground. These were seasoned soldiers, traveling quietly and confidently. All Justin could hear was the plod of hooves behind him and an occasional snort from one horse or another. His own horse traveled with sure, careful steps, although more slowly than when they had begun their long march.

Justin's fatigue was startled to alert wakefulness when his horse reared, its whinny piercing the still night air. Fighting to gain control of his horse, Justin did not notice the tall, shadowy form that moved out from the surrounding trees. A voice came on the wind. "Who goes there?"

Justin straightened abruptly, the reins dangling loosely from one hand as he spun toward the young man who now stood in full moonlight. "Fabian! What are you doing here at this hour?"

The young man shrugged in response, waving vaguely toward the forest behind him. "Care for some company on the last stretch of your travel?"

"That would be fine." Justin studied the group emerging from the darkness for a moment and then turned back to Fabian. "Where did you pick them up?"

"Twelve miles east of here. Holding a meeting around a sick man's bed." Fabian shook his head, his expression stoic as he watched the small group of men, women, and children gather next to the soldiers. "You'd think they would learn."

Justin did not answer. It was astonishing—all the tortures these Christians went through. Yet they showed no signs of giving up their faith. For this small assemblage, it would no doubt be the same. They would be facing death soon.

The Christians were silent, except for the cry of a baby from somewhere within the group. Justin watched them a moment longer, his heart constricting. Fabian had an iron will, a quality required for his business. Justin didn't think he could ever possess the same quality, which made him thankful he didn't have Fabian's job. To capture these peaceful people would prove too much for him to handle. They had committed no crime—at least, not in his eyes, though he knew the public would disagree with unrelenting fury.

Perhaps he was too weak—too soft. His own uncle, a senator, certainly thought so. But Justin had moved beyond caring what his uncle thought of him. Julian Gallus was a proud man, and no one could break through his shell.

But his own opinions about the Christians didn't really matter anyway. They would disappear from history soon, just like all the others. He could do nothing to help them.

.

PART ONE

CHAPTER ONE

Deep turquoise light seeped across the sky, announcing the dawn. Gusts of wind bearing the scent of sea air cooled Rachel Gallus's face as she turned from her dressing table and stepped toward the window. Perhaps she should stand on the balcony to enjoy the morning more fully. Some might not enjoy standing in the chilly air to see the morning sun glinting off the multi-colored leaves, but Rachel loved to immerse herself in the atmosphere of autumn.

Flinging a *palla*[1] around her shoulders to ward off the chill of the morning wind, she opened the door of her bedchamber and stepped out. Hues of lavender and soft rose tinted the eastern sky, spilling over the distant mountains at the edge of the sea far to the south. Rachel leaned out across the railing. The peristyle and formal

---

[1] Long, draped mantle or robe—traditional garment for Roman women.

gardens lay below, extending a welcome to visitors with its bay trees, paved walks, and fountains. Roses grew there during the summer, and a trellis of vines canopied a waterway. As part of the Senate among the patricians of Rome in the year A.D. 258, Rachel's father was wealthy and powerful. The family villa she had known as home for sixteen years stood out as one of the grandest in this part of the country.

"Rachel?"

The voice in the doorway behind her was so familiar that Rachel didn't turn around. "I didn't know you were up yet, Diana," she said as the other girl joined her.

"I couldn't sleep," answered Diana. "And when I saw the sunrise from my window, I thought I would probably find you here." Outsiders knew Diana as Rachel's personal slave, attending to her mistress's every need and whim; however, both girls knew that that their relationship held closeness and equality.

Diana leaned against the railing and stared toward the sea. "Sure is windy today," she commented. "Do you think it's going to rain?"

"That's what Father said." Rachel turned to face her for the first time. "Isn't this morning simply gorgeous?"

"You can say that again," murmured Diana. She glanced at her arm. "But look, I'm getting goose bumps."

"I like the chilly wind." Rachel smiled. "I could stay here all day."

Diana shivered and turned back to the door. "Not me. I think I'll go inside to stoke the fire."

"I can take breakfast in there," Rachel called after her. "Just bread and water, please."

As Diana vanished through the door, Rachel leaned

even farther over the railing, her gaze returning to the sky. Watching the sunrise always cast aside any melancholy lingering in her mood, breathing a promise of hope and freshness and better days ahead.

"How did they respond, Justin?"

The words jolted Rachel from her reverie. Startled, she stepped backward.

Her father was striding into the peristyle below, the purple stripe edging his white toga visible even in the dim light. Beside him walked her cousin Justin, one of the young Praetorians.[2] Though she could hardly see his face from this angle, there was no mistaking the thoughtful note in Justin's voice as he answered the senator.

"Calm—very calm, as though the death sentence didn't even startle them." He paused. "I can't understand it."

"It was all an act, my lad. All an act, as you should know already." The senator turned toward him. "Don't tell me you're getting soft, my boy," he said with an edge in his voice.

"They had absolutely no fear, Uncle Julian." Justin's voice quieted, as though thinking it through. "I couldn't help but wonder about it." He turned to face his uncle. "What have they done to deserve this, after all? Why should they not be free to serve whomever they choose?"

"They should not be free to serve whomever they choose because this is Rome and they must serve Rome and its emperor *only*. And you," Julian's voice rose, "will lead them to the arena today—personally. Do you hear me? Personally!" His features darkened with anger. "How many times have I warned you? You're playing with fire to

---

[2] Roman imperial bodyguards.

15

question our methods and philosophies. I will hear no more of this kind of talk—now or ever!"

"Yes, sir." The young soldier straightened tensely.

They walked in silence for a moment, and then Justin cleared his throat. "Sir?"

"What is it now?" The low voice was threatening, but Justin squared his shoulders and went on.

"I'm concerned about Aunt Cornelia and Rachel, sir. How will they respond when they discover that—"

"That's enough from you!" The senator pointed toward the entrance of the peristyle. "Our business is done. Leave at once!" Without waiting for an answer, he stalked off alone toward the gardens.

Rachel suddenly felt chilled. Gripping the railing until her knuckles turned white, she watched her father as he moved slowly into the gardens, his head bowed and his shoulders slumped as though carrying a heavy weight. What did this mysterious discussion mean? She could tell it had something to do with the hated sect of Christianity.

But she also knew beyond the shadow of a doubt that there was something more, something that struck deeper than the fact that Christians were being led to tortured deaths in the Colosseum's arena. Those types of deaths had been happening for quite some time. Perhaps the key to her father's dark moods recently lay in what she had just heard.   And only a few hours ago, Rachel had distinctly heard him crying out in his sleep. Never before had she known him to do that.

She thought of Justin's last words. *I'm concerned about Aunt Cornelia and Rachel, sir. How will they respond when they discover—* Discover what? His words were filled with ominous significance. Rachel turned, her fingers fumbling as she jerked open the door to her bedchamber.

Diana found Rachel sitting by the fire minutes later, staring absently into the blazing flame. "I thought you'd still be outside," she said in surprise, pausing in the doorway.

Rachel did not answer immediately. Standing up, she moved restlessly toward the window. Dawn was past the height of its glory now, and daylight had spread over the land. As she stood there, a robin flew by, its wings whistling as they caught the air current. Rachel watched the small bird swoop toward the forest beyond the peristyle walls. Then she spoke softly, as though to herself. "I wish I had wings so I could fly away from this place."

"If you're thinking about actually leaving," Diana said, "you may as well forget it. There's no way you could possibly just—go away."

"Perhaps not." Rachel glanced out the window again, listening to the birds singing merrily. "But I feel so stuck here that sometimes I wish I'd never been born."

"Rachel!" exclaimed Diana, almost under her breath.

But Rachel's black eyes were flashing now. "The questions I have about my past are overwhelming, and I don't have much hope of ever getting answers."

"But you can't go back now and change what happened," Diana said earnestly. "You have to make the best of the life you do know."

Rachel gave a short laugh. "Life—what is the purpose of it? Such an existence as this—the same routine day after day until it's an endless monotony that drowns ambition. I've begun to think I'll go mad! Do you know, Diana, I feel that in the sixteen years of my life, the only time I really *lived* was as a child. Ironic, isn't it? Mother says my future looks as bright as the sun. But if the future offers me only what it has offered her—" She stopped abruptly, her lips tightening as she turned away. "But there is no use in talking about it. Do you have breakfast ready?"

"Here it is." Diana looked doubtfully at the thin slice of bread. "Are you sure this is enough for you?"

"I'm never very hungry in the morning." Rachel shrugged and picked up the glass of water. "This is all I need."

"Most likely you'll scarcely eat anything at lunch, either," Diana pointed out.

"It'll tide me over 'til dinner." Rachel shrugged again. "I'm never hungry anymore."

Diana's soft black eyes riveted on Rachel with sudden intensity. "Does your mother know how you feel, Rachel?"

Rachel shook her head. "I would never tell her, Diana."

Diana set down her own glass of water. "Maybe you should. This question has been on your mind now for months. How much longer can you keep bottling it up inside?"

"It would never work," answered Rachel firmly. "Mother doesn't have the answer to my questions, and if she would know that I feel purposeless, it would only worry her. I don't think *anyone* knows the answer, Diana. Emperor Valerian himself would not be able to tell me my purpose in life, or why I am often unsettled inside. Why should I be discontent? I have all I need and could ever want." She glanced around the room, noting the rich tapestries and ornate sculptures. "I wonder if it's good for me. I feel so—so useless, Diana. Useless! No one needs me. How is it to be a slave? Do you feel fulfilled in your work?"

"I have the same questions," Diana acknowledged

thoughtfully. "But I'm so busy I scarcely have time to worry about them. I'd rather it be that way than to have too much time on my hands to think."

"Exactly!" Rachel nodded emphatically. "That's exactly what it is. I have too much time to ponder. My mind races in circles until I could scream." She shuddered. "It bothers me so much that I can't even sleep."

"Rachel?" Diana's voice was soft. "What was wrong with your father last night?"

Rachel closed her eyes, not wanting to think about the question. She stood up slowly. "Come with me, Diana." Opening the door, she led the way out to the balcony. "Watch my father down there in the gardens. He walks like a man carrying a heavy load. Something is on his mind—has been for a while now. And just this morning, I found out at least partly why." Swiftly she related the conversation she had overheard that morning, adding quietly, "Now I'm even more confused, Diana. I caught only a few threads of their discussion, and nothing fits together."

She paused and sighed. "At one time I would have known beforehand what it all means. Justin would've discussed it with me. We used to be close, even though Justin is two years older than I. But when he joined the Praetorians—" She paused, her eyes darkening. "Everything changed. Now we hardly even see each other, much less talk. I guess that's what time does to a person," she added in resignation. "We get older and things change. But I miss Justin. He was like the brother I never had."

Diana squeezed Rachel's arm gently. "Not everything has changed, has it?"

Rachel gave her a warm glance. "Our friendship will

never change, Diana. I only wish—" She halted as Diana held up a warning hand. Then she straightened her shoulders resolutely. "No, don't cut me off again. I've wished so many times that life would be different—that we could just be equals. Why shouldn't you be blessed with as many privileges as I have? Just because you were born in a different class—it isn't fair!"

"You know, most people would probably think you're out of your mind if they heard your opinions," Diana said dryly, her eyes returning to the figure of the gray-haired man still pacing agitatedly up and down the garden walks. "How many times do I have to tell you that life has made both of us what we are, and there's nothing we can do about it?"

"Someday that will change!"

Diana shrugged dismissively. Nodding toward the gardens where the senator still walked, she said, "What you overheard does sound strange, Rachel. But many Christians have died in the arena. Why should it be any different now?"

"That's what I can't figure out," answered Rachel. "Much less why he wouldn't have told my mother and me about it."

Diana furrowed her eyebrows. "Could the condemned ones be comrades from long ago?"

Rachel shook her head thoughtfully. "Father is a hard man, Diana. He would hardly remember old comrades with affection." Her forehead creased in thought. "I think it's something deeper," she said slowly. "Just what, I can't imagine. But he's nervous about it. Otherwise, why would he not tell us?"

Diana shivered slightly. "Maybe you should prepare

yourself, Rachel. Whatever it is, if this is anything to go by . . ." She left the sentence hanging.

Rachel didn't answer. After Diana went back inside, she watched alone from the balcony until her father finally left the peristyle. Her thoughts returned, haunting. *I wish I'd never been born. There are so many mysteries surrounding my life . . . And what Diana said: "But you can't go back now and change what happened. You have to make the best of the life you do know . . ."*

Diana knew as much as Rachel did about the events surrounding her early life. She knew about the discovery Rachel had made years ago that still plagued her with its untold secrets.

PARDON'S PRICE

CHAPTER TWO

Twelve-year-old Rachel loved to wander through the meadow during the magical hour of sunset and dusk. Every evening, bands of color reflected in the mirror of the lake as the long rays from the golden sun slipped toward the western edge of the world. The dreamy shadows would deepen into purple as the twilight breezes frolicked ahead of her dancing feet.

But this night was different. The wind neither laughed nor howled but seemed restless, rushing through forest groves until it sounded like an ocean. It whirled from the trees, sweeping down into the valley, the notes of its song winging away tremulously.

Rachel had wandered through the valley beside the lake for more than an hour when she heard a surprising sound. She looked around and noticed a slight girl about her own age kneeling amid the tall grasses and weeping. Shocked and concerned, Rachel bent down beside the girl. "What's wrong?" she asked.

The girl's head jerked up. She rose to her feet, her chest heaving as she hastily rubbed her eyes. "My sister died," she said, "and now her baby is alone because her daddy left and we don't know where he is. And we're too poor to keep the baby ourselves. Father said that another family will have to take care of her."

Rachel's eyes grew big. "That's awful! Do you know if you'll still be able to see the baby when she goes to live with someone else?"

"I hope so, but I don't know how far away she'll have to go," the other girl said, tears springing to her eyes again. "I miss my sister, and I can't stand the thought of her baby being an orphan."

Rachel could think of nothing to say in the face of the other girl's loss. Finally she said awkwardly, "I'm sure you'll find a good home for the baby."

As she walked home after that chance meeting, Rachel realized she hadn't even asked the girl's name; yet she felt a kinship in shared sorrow with her. Thinking she heard a chuckle of sinister glee in the wind, she glanced up at the sky, where the stars gleamed like cold, heartless gods. She shivered and shrank back. No doubt the shadow of death was even now stretching out its ghostly fingers to clutch the soul of another mother out there somewhere.

"Why do things like this happen?" Rachel asked during the evening meal. "Life is so cruel for some people. That poor baby! She'll never know her mother, and she'll be raised by someone who's not even from her family." She paused before adding thoughtfully, "I hope her new family will tell her where she came from and try to keep in touch with her birth family."

"I'm sure that baby will be adopted by good people," answered her mother gently. "But it might not be good for her to know about her birth mother. There might be shameful things about her family that she'd be better off not knowing."

Rachel's eyes widened. "But then—her parents would be lying to her because they wouldn't be telling her the truth about who she is! If I were that baby, I would want to know everything I could about my mother."

Something Rachel could not define flashed through her mother's dark eyes, sketching a troubled look on her features. "Let's hear no more of this discussion," her mother said quickly, turning away.

The senator, too, was frowning. "Do not bother yourself about this baby any longer," he said in a low voice. "It's a matter of no concern for a young girl like you."

Rachel was left staring from one to the other, a new apprehension in her eyes.

Until now, she had never questioned her life. She just accepted existence the way it was—beautiful and free. She enjoyed being with her family and friends, especially the villa's slaves. Theirs was an environment so different from the social world of her family, where she always felt so stiff and uncomfortable—bored with lady-like mannerisms. With the slaves she could be herself, having no fear of disapproval. Her personal slave, Diana, was her best and closest friend.

But now her parents' words had struck a warning that she couldn't shrug off.

PARDON'S PRICE

Strains of music followed Rachel as she slipped cautiously into the peristyle, pausing a moment just outside the atrium to listen. The light beat of footsteps behind the closed door assured her that various couples within were still dancing, thus providing the time she needed to escape from her fourteenth birthday party. When Mother discovered she was gone—well, she'd be far away by then, though a full explanation would certainly be in order later. But she couldn't worry about that now.

Only when she was through the peristyle entrance and on her way down the path in the woods did Rachel breathe more easily. So much was at stake here. She couldn't afford to let anyone know what she was doing. That in itself would be a disaster, not to mention her own misgivings, which grew with every step she took now that she was actually carrying out her plan.

Perhaps *plan* wasn't the right word. It was an impulsive decision, formed within a vortex of swirling emotions from what she had learned in the past hours of dinner. Just thinking back over the evening caused shiver.

———◆———

Rachel had found it hard to believe the tall girl in her reflection that night was actually herself. Excitement had kindled a radiant flash in her black eyes. Her new tunic of shimmering blue imported silk enhanced her clear olive skin and the lustrous gleam of her dark hair. The *cena*[3] that night was planned in honor of her birthday, and she felt unreservedly excited about it. Her father had

---

[3] Evening meal.

requested that she sing as entertainment for the guests—the first time he had ever asked her to do this, though she had dreamed of it for years. Now that she was fourteen, he seemed to realize she was no longer a child but a maturing young woman.

Her mother's recognition of this fact was clear in the necklace with a gold pendant, which she had presented to Rachel earlier that morning. It was the most expensive jewelry Rachel had ever owned. Now she fastened it carefully around her neck, admiring its brilliance in the glass.

"Rachel? Are you in here?" The door opened slowly, revealing the face of her friend Bernice peering around it. "Diana said you were still getting ready."

"You can't guess what happened," Rachel beamed, turning toward her.

"My father asked me to sing tonight for the guests! I was elated when he asked me. I thought it must be a happy dream. But it's real!" Breaking into laughter, she caught up the long, silky skirt of her tunic in one hand and danced around the room. "I'm so happy tonight, I feel as if I can't contain myself!"

If Rachel was expecting Bernice to share her joy, she couldn't have been more disappointed. Bernice only watched her silently, her eyes filled with concern. Rachel, at length stopping her spontaneous dance, looked quizzically into Bernice's eyes. Her eager words died on her lips, and she drew back slightly. "Bernice, is something wrong?"

Bernice shifted uneasily as troubled expressions chased across her face. "I was talking with my mother this afternoon," she began slowly. "I—I simply can't forget it.

Rachel, do you know—but how could you?" she murmured, as though to herself. "You've never mentioned it—it's hardly possible."

"What are you talking about?" Alarmed, Rachel noticed that Bernice was rubbing her hands together nervously. She looked hard at her friend.

Bernice dropped her gaze. "I could hardly believe it myself, but Mother said it's true. I thought you'd want to know—I know I would." She turned abruptly and grasped Rachel's shoulders, looking deeply into her eyes. "Rachel, your parents are not who you think they are. In fact, Julian and Cornelia aren't your parents at all."

"Not my parents!" She took a tiny step backward, staring at Bernice in disbelief. "What do you mean, they aren't my parents?" she demanded. "I've always known—they've always been—"

Bernice's grip on her shoulders tightened. "Secrets can be hidden for a long time."

"But Mother often talks about the day I was born," Rachel exclaimed. "I was born in their middle age, the child they thought they would never have. I was the joy of their lives, they told me."

"In a sense, what she said is true. She was there at the time of your birth because she is your grandmother." Bernice placed one hand on her arm as Rachel's head jerked up. "I know it's a difficult story to hear. But my mother knows the *truth.*"

Rachel made no answer. She straightened herself to her full height, standing tensely erect and still, her dark gaze riveted on Bernice. Her thoughts whirled. *There's always been a blank surrounding the time before I was born. Mother and Father have a way of evading the questions whenever I ask about it. Maybe this is the reason.*

"My mother was close friends with your mother and a girl called Adara back when the three were young," Bernice said at length, intently studying the fireplace. "Mother talked about the good times they had together, especially when they visited your mother. She was the only child of your grandparents, and they idolized her.

"My mother married a few weeks before your own mother did, but Mother said that as far as she knows, Adara never married. Adara moved away soon after that because her father's business failed, and Mother lost track of her—until your parents disappeared." Bernice turned to face Rachel, who was turning pale. "Mother says it's a mystery to this day what happened with your parents. You were just a tiny baby at the time, and your mother loved you dearly. Folks said a scandal must have been the cause of their disappearance, as if they fled capture or ridicule. No one ever knew the truth.

"Soon afterward, Adara came to visit my mother." Bernice was speaking in low tones, as though about to reveal a dark secret. "Mother discovered that Adara had been told in confidence what happened with your parents, but she would not betray the secret. Nothing has been heard about your parents since."

She met Rachel's eyes. "Mother said that at the time, some people were suspicious that your grandparents had something to do with your remaining behind—as though they worked behind your parents' backs somehow, and in the end you were left with them. Maybe it was because you were their first grandchild, the firstborn of their only daughter. Whatever happened then has long been forgotten by most people, but Mother said she doesn't think she could *ever* forget."

As Bernice fell silent, Rachel's face reddened. Everything she was saying fit the puzzle pieces together—the mystery she had sensed for quite some time. It had kept her awake many nights as she questioned and feared.

With a gesture of revulsion, Rachel tore the pendant necklace from her neck and flung it into a corner, grasping her tunic with the other hand at the same moment. Bernice watched in speechless horror as the beautiful garment fell in a haphazard heap on the floor. Rachel stared downward and raised her left foot high, her eyes black as midnight, her hands clenching so tightly the knuckles turned white.

"Rachel!" Bernice stifled a scream and sprang toward her, catching both arms and forcing her backwards. "Don't step on your tunic—you'll ruin it!"

"It's not mine," Rachel said coldly, wrenching free from Bernice's grasp. "It is Julian and Cornelia Gallus's possession—I want nothing to do with it."

"But everyone will know something is wrong if you show up with something else on." Bernice gathered the garment hastily in her arms and turned toward the dressing table. "Your necklace—at least it's still in one piece. Here, Rachel, quickly. Put on your tunic again, and I'll fasten the necklace around your neck. Whatever were you thinking?"

Rachel slipped slowly into her tunic again, the color returning to her face. She fastened a clear, steady gaze on Bernice as she whispered the words, "Does your mother know where Adara lives?"

Rachel escaped the party at last. A fierce wind tugged at her skirt, whipping it about her ankles and slowing her pace as she ran down the street. Reaching up, she wrapped her *palla* more securely about her head to protect her ears. No doubt her face would be a crimson shade by the time she returned home. Breathing hard, she came to a stop, uncertain of which way to go.

She had never been in this section of the city before, and she felt appalled at the run-down buildings that lined the *insula.*[4] In the gathering dusk she could see no farther than a few feet ahead. An uneasy chill crept over her spirit, subduing the expectant hope that had lent wings to her feet only seconds ago. Why had she chosen this hour to come?

But to go back to that festive gathering would also be difficult. How she had survived the evening, she did not know. With Bernice's words, her joy had vanished like a blown-out candle, leaving her heart a frozen shell that barred emotion, save for one burning desire.

Certainly no one else seemed to notice. When she sang, her voice soared, sweet and melodious as always, and every guest lavishly complimented her talent. But the praise fell on deaf ears. She had retreated into a solitary world where she felt like a phantom among the living, coming sharply out of it only when her grandparents beamed their pride upon her.

"Julian and Cornelia's beloved daughter," she had overheard one lady gushingly express. Rachel had never felt the likes of the anger she felt at that moment, even

---

[4] Multi-story apartment blocks.

worse than she had felt in her bedchamber when Bernice had told her the haunting story. A blinding fury made her want to scream in the lady's heavily painted face. In truth, Julian and Cornelia were nothing more than liars; their love for her as a daughter was a farce. She felt that she could never trust them again.

The *insula* came alive as a group of boys appeared around the corner ahead, their voices loud in the stillness of the night. A man staggered past without even glancing in Rachel's direction. Somewhere above her a window opened, and if Rachel had not heard it and stepped backward, the scrap remnants from a recent meal would have showered directly on her head. Rachel stared at the heap near her feet and shuddered. Yes, there *was* a fish head emerging from that disgusting mound, one eye gaping up at her. With another shudder, she turned away—straight toward the cluster of boys, who had silently formed a semicircle around her.

"What are you doing here?" demanded one of them. He stood half a head taller than the others, most likely the leader of the gang. "You don't live here, do you?"

Rachel shook her head, some of her fear receding as she glanced around. Most of the boys looked merely curious. Besides, she stood just as tall as the leader himself. Rachel had always disliked the fact that she was so much taller than other girls her age, but now she was suddenly glad for it.

"I'm looking for a woman whose name is Adara," she said, turning back to the tall boy. "I was told she lives somewhere in this *insula*. Do you know who she is?"

"There are lots of Adaras around here." The boy waved his arm in a wide arc and shot her a grin. "Maybe you're looking for that old crone who lives at the end of this street. We can take you there, all right."

All the boys were laughing now, enclosing Rachel in their midst as they began promenading toward the far end of the street. Confused, she tried to hold back. "I'm not looking for an old woman! I was told that Adara is younger than forty years old."

But the boys weren't listening. Rachel gave up trying to explain, growing more and more uneasy the farther they led her down the street. Her plan had seemed so reasonable when she first thought of it—even virtuous. But now it seemed merely foolhardy. She wished she could disappear.

"This way, girl." The leader grabbed Rachel's hand, half pulling her up a flight of stairs behind him. He walked with a swift, sure step through the filth that lined the steps, and Rachel felt herself recoiling, nearly gagging, as she realized what she was walking through—smelly remnants of meals, animal waste, and trash. This sort of clutter was never found where she lived. Desperately she glanced around, searching for a way—any way—to escape.

One of the boys walking close by dug his fingers into her arm. "What's the matter, girl?" he asked with the hint of a sneer. "Can't stomach it? Where are you from, anyway?"

Rachel drew back without answering, thankful now for the tattered *palla* she was wearing to hide her status. In this part of town, she wouldn't want to reveal that she was wealthy. She took a deep breath and lifted her head, squaring her shoulders. *I* will *go through with this. I must find Adara.*

"We're here to see Adara," the leader was telling an old man who had opened a door directly in front of them. He gripped Rachel's arm, pulling her forward. "This girl wants to see her, actually."

"You're here to see Adara?" The old man squinted at Rachel through the growing darkness. "That's my wife, and she can't get out of bed." The group leader had turned, his buddies joining him as he dashed down the steps. Before Rachel quite knew what had happened, she was alone with the old man—who certainly didn't appear to be any threat, the kind way he was smiling at her.

"Can't imagine what you'd want with my wife. She's pretty far gone. Now, if it's another Adara you're looking for, I know an Adara who used to live next door to us," he said. "Quite a woman she was, the kind you don't find too often nowadays, so kind and sweet! Never seemed to walk, but floated like she was on air. I thought it a right shame that she should be stuck in a place like this. She was too lily-white for it, too lily-white. Stayed at my wife's bedside when she took ill. Married a fine man later on and moved away. Was right sorry to see her go . . . yes, indeed, right sorry, but glad she could finally live somewhere she belonged. Heard she moved to the country—safest place for a woman like her."

"She moved?" Rachel hesitated. The old man's description sounded exactly like the person she was looking for.

"Been a number of years now, a number of years." The wrinkled man reached out, placing a claw-like hand on her shoulder. "I couldn't say what part of the country she is in now. But if you want to see my wife, I can take you to her. Just follow me."

Rachel took a deep breath, knowing that her search had come to a dead end with this information. She had no desire to see the elderly lady. She glanced back at the old man and smiled. "Thank you, but I think I'll just go home now."

"Not too many knew Adara Severus was even moving away," the old man said as she turned to leave. "So I don't think you'll get much help on that, no matter who you ask."

By the time she reached her home, Rachel had decided that her next step was to confront her grandparents. The closer she approached the villa, the more furious she grew.

All the guests had departed by the time she walked in through the atrium, and the rest of the villa—from the triclinium down the long hall to her grandfather's library—was empty. She paused just outside the library, discarding the tattered *palla* before she opened the door. With the aromas from the street still clinging to it, it would be impossible to hide where she had been.

Her grandfather was seated at his high desk, writing with a stylus that moved swiftly across the scroll's page. He glanced up as Rachel stood framed in the doorway. Turning toward her, a slight frown appeared beneath bushy gray brows.

"Where were you, Rachel?" he demanded. "Your mother and I discovered awhile ago that you were no longer with us in the triclinium. I was about to go in search of you." He paused before remarking dryly, "Only a child needs to be reminded of rules for her own safety. I can see by your red cheeks that you were outside, my girl; you know the danger of leaving the villa after dark." Concern edged his tone now. "By all appearances you are safe and sound—is that truly so?"

Rachel hardly heard him. Closing the door behind her, she walked confidently toward her grandfather's desk. "I have a question to ask you," she said without preamble.

He leaned back in his chair. "Something important, is it?"

"I want you to tell me everything you know about my parents, Grandfather," announced Rachel deliberately.

His eyes widened. "What?"

"My parents," Rachel said firmly. "You lied to me all these years, saying that you are my father, and that your wife is my mother. I have every right to ask you for the truth now."

Her grandfather's mouth worked, but no sound came.

"And now I'm left floundering," Rachel went on boldly. "My whole life has been a sham. I don't know who I am!" Tears stung her eyes, but she held them back by sheer force of will and concentrated fully on her grandfather. "Who are my parents? What happened that they have disappeared? Where are they now? Why was I left behind? Tell me the truth!"

As Rachel flung the last words into the air, her grandfather, surprisingly swift and agile for his age, leaped to his feet. "Enough!" he roared. "You will never speak of this again, do you hear me? Never!" His fist came down on the desk so hard the surface rattled. "Neither will you speak of this to your mother! It is a closed issue! Do you understand me? It is closed!"

Rachel stared at him. Never before had she heard that note of rage in her grandfather's voice, or observed the hot color that stained his features a mottled purple. As he strode around the desk, she turned abruptly and left the room, pausing at the door for a final word. "I'll never forgive you for this!"

"Rachel—Rachel Gallus!"

Her grandfather reached the door just as it slammed in his face.

Pardon's Price

CHAPTER THREE

Two years didn't make much of a difference. Rachel still felt like the girl of the past whose world had crashed down around her. Never had she felt so alone as she listened to the conversation between Justin and her grandfather. "Something is wrong, no doubt about that," she whispered. "I feel just like I did when I first found out about my parents—that sinking feeling of being out of control. If I could only know what the future holds!"

By mid-morning the temperature had dropped sharply, and strong winds were whipping dark clouds rapidly across the sky. The first drops of an icy rain started to fall as the throng crowding the street moved toward the temple, where sacrifices would be held before the afternoon entertainment at the Colosseum. Thunder boomed low in the distance.

"That was more than thunder," Rachel's grandmother murmured, lifting dark eyes that held a troubled look as they gazed over the city. "Did you hear the lions? They are raging with hunger . . ."

"Mother, please." Rachel placed a hand on the older woman's arm and squeezed it gently. "Don't say that here. Not now." She looked around uneasily for her grandfather. Noting that he was walking some distance behind them as he spoke with another senator, she breathed a sigh of relief. Julian had no patience with his wife when she spoke in that haunted way.

The closer they approached the temple, the more agitated the people became. Already there was a small crowd at the doors, pushing and shoving to enter first in order to gain a good view of the sacrificial rituals. Even Cornelia adapted to the spirit of the throng, seeming to lose her uneasiness.

Rachel looked around uneasily as she stepped into the temple. *There's something going on here—something that have been afraid of for a long time. It's like there's an evil presence hovering over the altar of Jupiter. I don't feel at all comfortable—why people go into a frenzy about this is beyond me.* She looked at the bearded statue carved from stone. Jupiter's cold face was painted red in observance of the festivity dedicated to him. *He is so repulsive. I wish there were a god who was kind and would bless those who worship him. I would believe in that god. What I wouldn't give to get out of here!*

She glimpsed Diana, directly across the room among other slaves. She was gazing toward the massive altar with a blank expression. When she turned slightly, her eyes met Rachel's. The expressions each read in the other told them their feelings were mutual.

"Rachel! Wait for me!"

Swept along in the midst of a mob swarming to the temple doors, Rachel glanced back as she tried to stop. The slim brunette pushing her way through the crowd stood taller than average, something about her demeanor commanding respect. Athena had always been like that—a strength cloaking her personality that honed her natural femininity. But now her smile flashed even brighter than the jewelry lining her ears and arms, and her eyes sparkled as she caught Rachel's arm. "Be sure you sit with me at the Colosseum today, Rachel. I have something to tell you."

"She's fairly bursting with this secret," Bernice added, stepping around Athena. "Acts like she can hardly wait to get to the Colosseum."

"Why am I not surprised?" Rachel teased, knowing of Athena's fascination with gladiators. "You used to hate that place, though."

"You're a good one to talk," Athena retorted, tossing her head. "I left my childhood terrors of the Colosseum behind long ago—but I'm not so sure about you."

"Oh, I left my terrors behind long ago, too," Rachel assured her, more quickly than the occasion required.

"It's something everyone goes through as a child, I suppose," Bernice said. "Eventually we get over it, of course. Of the Colosseum and the Circus Maximus,[5] I'm not sure which I prefer now."

"The Colosseum, of course," exclaimed Athena. "No question in my mind. I'd go there every day if I could."

Rachel shot her friend a sideways glance. She had never understood Athena's feelings about the Colosseum, though

---

[5] Chariot-racing stadium.

she knew the sports held an intoxicating pleasure for many who attended. For herself it was—no, she wouldn't think of that now.

"I used to be really scared of it," Bernice said with a chuckle. "Sometimes I begged my mother to take me home."

"That sounds like my little niece," said Athena. "Just yesterday, she—" Rachel tuned Athena out as her eyes focused on the amphitheater in the distance, towering toward the sky like an unconquerable fortress. She felt the familiar fear clutch her heart and took a deep breath. *Get over it, Rachel Gallus,* she told herself fiercely. *You told the girls that you left your childhood terrors behind long ago—now don't let them see how you feel at this age!*

Rachel's grandfather found her just as the girls were about to enter the corridors of the Colosseum. "Where is your mother?" he questioned, breathing heavily. His face was pale, and the expression in his eyes alarmed her.

"I just talked to her," Rachel said, watching him closely. "She's out there somewhere." Turning to Athena, she said, "You girls go on."

"We'll be waiting for you," responded Athena, turning away.

"Rachel." The senator moved toward the arched columns that overlooked the gallery below, gazing across the vast area for a long moment. "I want you to sit with your mother today," he said at length, appearing to speak to the rapidly filling seats rather than to her. He turned abruptly and strode away without another word, leaving Rachel to stare after him.

What a strange request. Never before had he cared where she chose to sit when she came here, much less appointed the position. She stepped forward to ask him why, but as he disappeared down the corridor, her query drowned in the sea of humanity around her.

———————◆———————

Her grandmother was surveying the arena as Rachel approached. She did not stir until Rachel touched her shoulder. At the touch, she jumped. "Rachel! I thought you were sitting with your friends."

"I was planning to. But Father asked me to sit with you."

"He did?" Cornelia looked at her quizzically, and Rachel shrugged her shoulders. "I don't understand it either. But you look like you should be in bed, Mother. Has your heart been giving you trouble again?"

"My heart is fine," Cornelia answered sharply. A grin tugged at Rachel's lips.

"A Roman never admits the truth," she said, sitting down beside her grandmother. "I want to know how you're really feeling." Cornelia turned away without replying, and Rachel studied her for a moment.

For as long as she could remember, her grandmother had struggled with a heart condition the doctors kept expecting to worsen. Events such as this seemed to trigger heart trouble, but never badly enough that her grandparents asked her to stay close by. So why was her grandfather commanding it now?

"He's pretty good," Cornelia commented, tipping her head slightly. Rachel followed her gaze to where a young boy was entering the arena below, standing straight and tall on two horses, one foot on each horse, as he coolly surveyed the throngs. He was the leading act in the parade that would begin the day.

The minutes from then on seemed to fly. The fights opened with a long line of men marching into the arena, armed only with nets and spears to meet wild lions, tigers, and boars charging from their cages. Rachel felt like covering her eyes. This fight involved various beasts kept in their cages for days without food and water. When turned out into the arena, they became fiends raging with hunger.

A thunderous roar of applause from the stands resounded around the Colosseum, but Rachel shuddered and refused to join the cheering. Had she been at liberty to leave, she would gladly have done so immediately. Men and beasts were dropping one after another, filling the sand with blood and the air with screams of the wounded. With a gasp, she squeezed her eyes shut.

"Rachel Gallus!" someone cried merrily, causing Rachel to open her eyes. "You surely won't sleep through the fight of the gladiators, will you?"

Startled, Rachel turned to find Athena standing next to her. "Where did you come from?" she exclaimed in surprise. "I thought you were with the other girls!"

"When you didn't come back, I decided to join you. Surely you won't object, will you?" Athena pushed a long strand of hair out of her eyes as she dropped down beside Rachel. "I wanted to talk with you." Rachel raised an eyebrow, and Athena leaned closer. "I've been wanting to tell you all week, and I can't wait any longer."

"Don't you dare tell me—" interrupted Rachel, grasping her arm. "You *didn't* speak with that gladiator Cadmus again, did you?" She gazed into the girl's dancing eyes and shook her head. "Athena!"

"You haven't heard everything, Rachel," laughed Athena. "Just listen to this. If Cadmus wins his fight in the arena today, he will receive his *rudis.*[6] Rachel, think of it! We'll be free to marry!"

"Your father will never allow it," answered Rachel coolly. "He loathes Cadmus, and he won't change his mind even after Cadmus is free."

Athena tossed her head. "I'm not worried about that. If Father refuses to accept Cadmus into his favor even after he's free, he'll change his mind in time. You'll see."

"You mean—" Rachel gasped. "You would elope?"

"We see no other choice, Rachel." Athena studied her intently. "Tell me, why do you dislike Cadmus so?"

"I want what's best for you, Athena. And for a husband, I think you could do far better than marrying Cadmus."

"But *why?*" Athena persisted, her face puckered into a frown.

Rachel felt her face flush. She couldn't understand what Athena saw in Cadmus. She felt he was nothing more than a bully, resorting to violence to get what he wanted. She saw Athena taking on some of the same characteristics as she spent more time with Cadmus.

But she couldn't tell that to Athena. "It's not that I dislike him," she evaded. "He just seems—rough. Has he asked you to run away with him?"

"He knows as well as I do how Father feels about him. But he won't let Father stop him from marrying me—and neither will I."

That's exactly what I mean, Athena, Rachel wanted to

---

[6] A wooden sword signifying freedom.

say. *He has changed you into a girl who will stop at nothing to get what she wants.* "Listen, Athena," she said softly. "If that's what you have your mind set on doing, no one will stop you. Think carefully before you do it. That's all I can say."

"Cadmus says his life has changed because of me." Athena lowered her eyes, long lashes sweeping her cheeks as the color deepened in them. "I'm what has kept him from going completely insane in that training school for the gladiators." She took a deep breath. "I'm glad of it, too, Rachel. Cadmus had no idea what he was getting into when he started training, and the love between us has saved him from becoming a brutal beast. If *you* could help a man this way, wouldn't you do it?"

Rachel had never thought of it like that before. She glanced back toward the arena, where columns of gladiators was marching into it from the far side. "If Cadmus earns his freedom tonight, Athena," she murmured, "I'll be happy for you."

The gladiators halted before the Emperor's box, raising their right hands to Valerian in a salute. "Hail, Emperor! We who are about to die salute you!"

Normally Rachel dreaded the gladiatorial combat. But now she watched intently, noting that Cadmus, a brawny young giant, was fighting with a sword and shield. He had a good chance of winning his freedom, no doubt about that.

The battle among the gladiators was swift and fierce, escalating the response of the spectators into frenzied excitement. Athena caught Rachel's hand as Cadmus was struck down, gripping it so tightly that Rachel nearly cried out in pain. Using all his strength, which was waning quickly from loss of blood, Cadmus lifted his left arm, appealing for mercy from the multitude. Instantly, thumbs went down everywhere, while yells of, "Get him! Kill him! Away with him!" became a thunderous roar resounding around the Colosseum.

Emperor Valerian gazed over the gallery and resolutely gave the thumbs-down sign. The conquering gladiator did not waste a second. He drove his trident into Cadmus's chest and rendered death to the young giant with one final blow.

Athena collapsed against Rachel without a sound, her face deathly white and her eyes dilating with anguish. Rachel held her tightly, feeling as though she could scream at the top of her lungs and vent her fury against this bloodthirsty throng. They were no better than brutal beasts themselves.

Without warning, Athena sprang up and rushed blindly from the gallery, heading toward the corridor. Rachel, already half-rising from her seat, was stopped by Cornelia's hand on her arm. "Let her go, Rachel," she said quietly. "She needs to be alone."

"You're right," Rachel agreed reluctantly. "I'll go to her later."

The rest of the fights passed in a blur, clearing only when a column of men, women, and children filed into the arena. Rachel leaned forward, her whole body tensing. No doubt these people were Christians, sentenced to death in the arena for their faith. This faith had become a topic of much discussion among the Roman citizens when the Christians' refusal to conform to the state religion under the Emperor's command had shocked the public and enraged the authorities. Valerian had issued a decree demanding that all the Christians who would not conform be hunted, captured, and killed as punishment. Their peculiar beliefs were cloaked with secret practices that many believed to present a threat against the Empire. Countless Christians had already suffered, willing to lay down their lives rather than renounce their beliefs.

Her grandfather in particular seemed to despise these people. He attended conferences with the Emperor and Roman Senate frequently, not hesitating to share his opinions on what should be done with the Christians. More than once Rachel had lain awake long into the night, wondering why he was so opposed to them. She never tired of watching them in the arena. There was something so joyful in the way they faced death, something so peaceful that was never found in the deaths of other men who faced the turned-down thumbs with a screaming agony of fear. The Christians seemed to face death with something calmer than terror and stronger than resignation. Sometimes they actually smiled when they faced death in the arena.

A short column of Christians filed into the arena below —only thirteen in all. The day before there had been sixty who had been killed here, either burned or thrown to the beasts. A few weeks before, a total of one hundred had been thrust into the arena in two days. But these Christians were only a handful out of their actual number, according to Rachel's grandfather.

Rachel's attention focused on the man leading the line of prisoners. He was the tallest one of them all, appearing to be in his mid-thirties, walking with a firm, purposeful step toward the center of the arena. A young woman walked at his side, her head barely reaching his shoulder, a radiant joy shining from within. Rachel caught her breath as she noted the woman's serene beauty.

"Now thanks be to God, who always makes us triumph in Christ!" The man's booming shout brought a hush to the whole multitude. "He has redeemed us with His blood, washing us whiter than snow, and we are about to join Him in glory forever!" His words appeared directed toward the Emperor's box and the Roman Senate nearby, still as statues in their seats. "All of heaven will rejoice when we enter glory!"

As loud cries of anger against his words rose from the crowd, the beasts' cages were opened, allowing lions and tigers to enter the arena from the far side. One large tiger, so lean that ribs showed through its tawny skin, bounded toward the man standing in the center of the arena, unleashing its fury in a roar that reverberated against the walls of the Colosseum. Within minutes, nothing was left of its target but pools of blood, shreds of clothes, and mangled flesh and bones.

Rachel gulped, fighting nausea. The beautiful woman next to the man went down under the force of a lion slamming into her body. A small child darted ahead of another lion, screaming in fright. He fell as the cruel claws of the lion tore into his shoulders. The crowd bellowed in response, rising to their feet as one. Rachel covered her eyes and turned away.

It was then that she noticed her grandmother falling headfirst onto the stone floor.

PARDON'S PRICE

CHAPTER FOUR

Your grandmother is asking for you, Rachel." Diana stood in the doorway as Rachel looked up from the scroll on which she was writing. She stepped forward, her eyes filling with compassion at the frightened look in Rachel's dark eyes. "She's in grave danger, Rachel, and the physician is afraid that she will not live."

Rachel's face blanched. "Wait for me here, will you?"

Diana squeezed Rachel's hand, her tone low. "I will."

After Rachel's footsteps had faded down the hall, Diana remained standing motionless, her eyes shadowed with concern. At length she stepped out into the hallway and spoke to the figure waiting in the shadows. "You still wish for me to tell her?" she asked softly.

"By all means." Moonlight illuminated the bronzed face of her cousin and fellow slave Mario as he stepped into the room. "It's only fair, Diana."

"Are you sure she will think so?"

"We'll have to take the risk." Mario studied her eyes, and his own sobered.

"Trust me, Diana. Something tells me she needs to know."

"I know," Diana sighed. "But I dread telling her."

Mario spoke compassionately. "But you need to. And I'm going to go get the horses ready."

Diana's eyes widened. "Oh, Mario! Really?"

"We have to be prepared," he said quietly. "You know how she is, Diana." He disappeared from sight down the hallway.

The events at the Colosseum the day before had been replaying themselves over and over in Rachel's mind.

In that terrible moment of revulsion, she had slumped back in her seat, only to find her grandmother in a deathlike faint, one hand clutching her chest. From his seat in the Senate, her grandfather had noticed what was happening, and he rushed through the aisles until he reached them. "Get the physician," he barked at Rachel, lifting his wife into his arms. "I'm taking her home."

A day had passed as Cornelia lay silently in her bed, the physician hovering over her. Rachel had only been allowed to peek in on her grandmother once. To pass the time, she had slipped upstairs to her bedchamber, where she lingered on the balcony.

"I usually love my balcony," she had written in the scroll where she kept her journal. "It is here that I can watch the day slide in and out, gaining peace from the nature surrounding me—what little peace there is to gain in it. But I'm beginning to feel sure that there is no such thing as peace in all the world—for anyone."

She was doubly sure of that now as she ran down the stairs, her throat tight with fear. Pausing on the landing, she discovered the door of her grandmother's chamber slightly ajar and the physician disappearing in the other direction toward the atrium. From within the room came her grandmother's voice, high, shrill, and accusing.

"How could you do this, Julian Gallus?"

"You must understand something, Cornelia." Through the open door, Rachel saw her grandfather bend closer to his wife. "They were *Christians*—it was only what they deserved."

"It was your own daughter and son-in-law!" Cornelia cried out. "How *could* you find it in your heart to send Elisabetta and Marcellus to the arena? If Rachel knew of this, it would kill her!"

"I didn't send them," he began.

"Justin told me you were behind it all, Julian." The words were cutting, her eyes flashing as they locked with her husband's. "And you even assigned Justin to lead the Christians to the arena. I thought Fabian always does that."

He shifted slightly. "He needs to learn sometime, Cornelia."

Cornelia wasn't listening. "Would you do that to me if I became a Christian?" Heavy silence filled the room, broken only by the sound of heavy breathing.

Rachel stood frozen on the landing, incapable of speech or movement. Had she heard correctly?

At length her grandfather spoke, his voice weary and old. "I don't think anything will be gained by going further with this discussion. We need to leave it a closed issue."

As he turned around, Rachel sprang back silently, disappearing into the shadows. He must not find her here, listening to every word of the conversation.

All the way up the stairs, the horrifying realization whirled through her brain. *The people who died in the arena yesterday were my parents!*

Diana was dusting the room when Rachel burst in and flung herself across the bed, burying her face in the pillow. "I hate him, Diana. I *hate* him!" She sat up, her eyes burning with anger. "My own grandfather! He has no heart, no mercy! I hate him!"

"What are you talking about, Rachel?" Diana asked quietly.

"Do you remember the couple who died in the arena yesterday? Remember the man who spoke to the crowds with a voice like a trumpet before he died?" Rachel's eyes blazed like dancing flames as she spoke, crimson color flushing her cheeks. "Diana, that man was my father. My *father!* And the beautiful woman beside him was my mother. Two innocent humans, torn to pieces by the lions—all on account of my grandfather's hatred and pride. I know now why he despises the Christians so—my parents became Christians those long years ago. I don't know the whole story yet, but it's coming together."

Diana nodded. "I know, Rachel," she said heavily.

Rachel stared at her friend. "But—what? How did—?"

"Mario just told me a little bit ago. I was going to tell you soon."

Rachel slid out of bed and crossed the room, where she clasped Diana's hands in her own. "I know my grandfather is a hard man, but he's also known as a just, fair man. What possessed him to do this?"

"Perhaps he didn't want to do it," suggested Diana softly.

"What do you mean?" Rachel stared at her.

"He's been having a hard time this past week, you know. Not able to sleep at night . . . perhaps he didn't want to do this, but his pride kept him from stopping the chain of events."

"His pride is greater than his love," Rachel spat out the words. "I've known that all my life. And his pride won again this time." She paused, staring into the fire. "Or perhaps it goes deeper than that. Was my grandfather always like this? When my parents first became Christians, how did he respond? Something made him bitter and angry—and I tend to think it started then. So many questions—and no answers!"

Diana gave her an empathetic look. "But in contrast, your parents weren't bitter."

"No. And that's another big puzzle." Firelight danced across Rachel's hair as she lowered her head. "The words my father spoke in the arena . . . I can't forget them. He said something about living in glory—that all of heaven would rejoice upon their arrival. What is glory? What is heaven? And this god they believe in—is he anything like the gods we worship?"

"I don't think so," Diana said slowly. "They believe their god is alive, in the sense that he sees everything and hears their prayers."

Rachel stood up, pacing toward her window. "The men who die in the arena are afraid—the gladiators, the men who fight the beasts. They often cry out to their gods, but it doesn't get them anywhere; they still die in fear. And what happens then?

"But the Christians seem to have so much . . . assurance. Peace. That's what it is! Oh, the children cower in fear, but the adults—if they're afraid, they certainly don't show it." She spun around to face Diana. "I don't think it's a front. I've seen it too often to believe that it isn't real. Whatever those people believe, they have confidence in it. I wish I could have talked with my parents before they died, Diana. I would've asked them a lot of questions."

There was silence between the girls for a long moment. At length Diana drew a breath. "What makes you think that both your parents are dead?"

Rachel's eyes widened. "You saw them die, didn't you?"

Diana shifted slightly and squared her shoulders. "There's something else I need to tell you, Rachel. Do you recall how your grandfather left right after breakfast this morning and didn't get back until tonight, after the *cena* was over?" Without waiting for an answer, she went on, her words faster now. "Your grandfather asked Mario to go with him to the country to visit a woman who was asking to see him on her deathbed. And so, Rachel, your grandfather traveled to visit—his daughter."

"His daughter?" Rachel's voice squeaked.

"Your mother," confirmed Diana softly. "She was not killed in the arena as it appeared. The Christians often sneak into the Colosseum for the bodies of their dead and take them to the catacombs to bury them. They found your mother still alive, but barely. They rushed her away to save her life, but Mario said that the physician believes she has only a week, at the most, to live."

She paused, her gaze meeting Rachel's hesitantly. "Mario and I thought you should know, Rachel. Your mother wanted to see your grandfather and try to make peace one more time. He agreed to it—under one condition. If she gave up her faith, peace would be restored, and she'd also have the privilege of meeting you." Diana shook her head. "Whatever this faith of the Christians is, it gives them amazing strength, Rachel. Your mother refused to give up her faith, even though it meant never seeing you again."

Rachel took a deep breath. "I have to go see her."

Diana's brows furrowed. "Really, I don't think you should."

"I *must*," repeated Rachel calmly. "I need to somehow disguise—"

"Rachel, think!" Diana clutched at Rachel's sleeve. "You shouldn't go at this time of the night. Do you have any idea how far it is?"

"It doesn't matter to me," Rachel said quietly. "I am going to my mother, and nothing is stopping me. I'd find a way to go even if my grandfather explicitly forbade it! My mother and I have been separated for nearly sixteen years. Do you think I'm going to let anything stop me from seeing her once—*just once*—before she dies?"

"Rachel!" Diana grabbed both her arms and spun her around. "It's too dangerous for you to go now. You will have to go through dark streets and alleys, where there are gangs of thieves and pickpockets. You could be robbed, assaulted—or killed! It's too dangerous—you can't go alone!"

"If I have to, I will," Rachel said steadily. "I must go *now*. If I wait until morning, I might be too late."

Diana sighed. "Well, then, I will help you. I'll try to find you some old clothes." She left the room without another word. Rachel waited until her footsteps had faded before slipping silently into the hall that led to her grandfather's study.

The spacious room was empty, with a fire crackling in the hearth. Her heart pounding, Rachel stood still at the door and listened. She could not hear anything, but she had to be quick in what she wanted to do. Her grandfather could come at any moment.

Stepping inside, Rachel sat at the desk and placed her hand on the knob of a drawer. As she did so, a large shadow appeared on the door. For a moment her heart nearly stopped, her feet frozen in place. She glanced about frantically, searching for a place to hide. The sofa next to the hearth seemed much farther away than two feet as she sprang toward it. She knelt down behind it and waited, her breath searing her chest from the effort of holding it in.

Her grandfather entered the room, talking over his shoulder. "Come in and take a seat, Justin," Rachel heard him say.

"Thank you, Uncle Julian, but I have no desire to be seated," answered Justin. "And I realize that I could have waited until morning, but I have plans of leaving the city tomorrow. I'd rather go ahead and talk with you now."

The sofa creaked as the senator settled into it, and Rachel could only hope the shadows would hide her if he chose to look behind it. "I presume you have received the Emperor's orders?" he asked.

"Yes, sir." Justin's shadow was pacing now, looming high on the wall above Rachel and then receding as he turned. "You know about it?"

"Indeed." The senator paused a moment, as though watching the young soldier closely. At length he spoke again. "You seem disturbed."

"I just have questions, that's all," answered Justin a bit forcefully. "Why is the Emperor promoting me to this position of finding the Christians in the catacombs?"

"The Emperor has been quite impressed with your conduct and has decided that you were the one most eligible." The senator paused before adding pleasantly, "In fact, you have me to thank for this honor. I suggested you for the position."

Justin's shadow halted abruptly. "You suggested me?" His tone was low, with something in it that made Rachel cringe.

"Indeed I did." The senator's shadow leaned forward slightly. "The final decision, of course, was up to Emperor Valerian, but we both feel that you have proved yourself worthy of this position. Finding the Christians in the catacombs will be no easy task, we realize; but the Emperor is determined to teach those fools a lesson they will not soon forget." His chuckle sounded more like a snarl. "They'll learn they can't get away with their crazy ideas, and that their god is a lie."

"I am—in charge?" Justin nearly whispered the words.

"The head officer," the senator verified. His voice softened. "You must get rid of these notions that Christians can serve whomever they please, my lad. They are disobedient to the law and a threat to the Roman Empire. Their numbers are increasing, and we must stop their influence before it gets worse. They are dangerous, and whoever follows them is doomed for death."

For a long moment Justin did not answer. At length he straightened, his shadow a tall silhouette against the fire. "And if I refuse this?"

Bristling, the older man rose to his feet. "If you refuse, you'll lose your only chance of a position in which everyone regards you with the highest esteem. You will become a disgrace to your family and the entire army! Are you actually refusing?"

Silence hung heavy in the room, broken only by the crackling of the flames.

At last Justin lowered his head, resignation evident in the movement itself. "I only wished to question you about this, sir. When do I begin?"

Much as Rachel wished she could tune out the rest of the conversation, every word fell on her ears like burning sparks. With the plans the senator and his nephew were developing, she knew it was imperative to go through with her plan to meet her mother—this very night. She might never have the chance again.

Chapter Five

I t's a good thing it's cold tonight," Rachel said to Diana, without turning from her reflection in the glass. "I wouldn't be able to hide my long hair if I had no excuse to wear this hooded cloak."

Diana shifted restlessly and crossed to the window. "That's right. You need to look as much like a man as possible. It's so dangerous out there. Do you really have to go?"

"I've never been more sure of anything in my life, Diana," answered Rachel with quiet finality. "I should think you would understand, since you've been separated from your mother too."

Diana lowered her head. "It's different for you. My mother lives all the way back in Greece. When my father died, she couldn't afford to feed all of us, and she made arrangements for me to live with relatives, who then sold me as a slave. The day I left my mother's house, I turned around to wave goodbye, and she had already gone back inside and shut the door."

"That's what you always say, but—Diana, she was your *mother!*" Rachel faced her earnestly. "Surely no mother is that unfeeling toward her child!"

Diana shrugged. "Mother was never one given to affection. I don't know what she was thinking. But whenever I think of finding her, I think of her coldness, and then I know I don't want to find her. For you, it's different."

Rachel straightened slowly. "Is it? My mother refused to give up her faith, even to meet me. What kind of faith separates you from your own family?"

"But you still believe she loves you," Diana pointed out. "You've seen enough of the Christians to know that your mother will receive you with open arms."

"That's true," answered Rachel. "I do believe they're good people. I've never believed the rumors that they're cannibals. In the arena they're so peaceful and joyful. They never fight with the authorities when they're captured and taken to prison. I want to know what makes them so fearless."

Diana's expression darkened. "I still wish you'd listen to me about traveling all that way tonight, Rachel. You don't even know how to get there!"

"I'll find Mario and ask him," answered Rachel. "I'll wake him if I have to. Don't worry about me, Diana. I'll ride my mare. I'll be able to outdistance any danger with Princess. She runs like the wind, you know."

"Be careful. That's all I ask," whispered Diana.

"Miss Rachel. I thought you would come."

Rachel stopped in her tracks, the air leaving her lungs. Mario was standing just inside the stable doors. "I have my horse ready," he added.

"Ready for—for what?" Rachel stammered.

"You surely weren't thinking of going alone," answered Mario calmly. "You don't know the way, and it's too dangerous—especially at this hour. I'm going with you." He vanished into the shadows and reappeared in a moment, leading two horses by their bridles. "You ride Princess and stay close to me."

"But I don't want to get you in trouble," Rachel protested.

"Wait to say that until we're going through those dark alleys, and then I'll believe you," Mario retorted. "I only hope I won't need to use this dagger."

Without comment, Rachel whipped out a dagger from her own garments and held it up. "From my grandfather's study," she explained in answer to the startled query in Mario's dark eyes. "I'm ready. Let's go."

He glanced at her curiously, as though seeing her for the first time. "You're brave, you know that?"

"Do I pass as a boy?" she returned, glancing down at her disguise.

He grinned and bowed. "You nearly deceived even me, Miss Rachel."

The night was still, with only a sliver of moon in the inky sky. They rode in silence, and Rachel tensed in the saddle, her thoughts racing and tumbling in a whirlpool of confusion. Only one thought surfaced clearly—a thought that spilled out before she checked it.

"How did my mother act toward my grandfather when

he refused to let her see me?"

Mario's answer was immediate, as though he'd been expecting the question.

"I'm sure she was disappointed, but her belief in the god she serves is so great that she was able to accept it calmly." He turned to face her. "You have strong parents, Rachel. I wouldn't be surprised to hear that your father was a teacher among the Christians."

"I've heard of their leaders," Rachel said thoughtfully. "They stand firm in their beliefs. And they're the ones our government seems to hate particularly."

They were nearing an *insula* now, situated in one of the poorest sections of the city. Rachel remembered the night when she was fourteen and had visited an *insula* much like this one in search of Adara. The memory held a bitter edge. It brought questions she had no way of answering, and it widened the breach between herself and her grandparents each time she thought of it. Fury tightened her hands on the reins. *It's not right that my grandparents never told me the truth—it's just not fair!*

She sensed Mario shifting his position next to her as he slowly reached for his dagger. Her glance fell on a group of men lounging around the street corner they were approaching. As they drew nearer, Mario turned toward her. "Move to the other side of me," he whispered out the side of his mouth.

Rachel obeyed, her fingers clutching her own dagger until her knuckles turned white. The men were talking and laughing loudly. Perhaps they could pass by without even being noticed. She bent low and kneaded her hands along her horse's neck. The graceful bay mare responded, settling into a canter that led her safely past the ruffians.

When at last Mario lashed his horse into a full gallop with his whip, Princess lengthened her stride on her own accord. Rachel began to relax for the first time since starting out.

"I can depend on you to get me there safely, can't I, Princess?" she whispered into the flickering ears. Princess tossed her head and whinnied in response, her stride ever lengthening.

It took three hours to reach their destination. By then, Rachel was thoroughly exhausted, both from lack of sleep and mounting tension. It was already past midnight.

A tall youth of about fifteen years met them just outside the stables. "We've been expecting you," he said as Mario swung to the ground. "We have a roaring fire inside to take the chill from your bones."

Rachel, already standing on the ground, glanced up in surprise. "You've been *expecting* us?"

The two boys glanced at each other before the tall youth turned and met her gaze evenly. "You are Elisabetta's daughter, right?"

"Yes, but I—" Confused, Rachel looked from one to the other.

Quickly Mario said, "They'll take care of the horses, Rachel. Let's go inside."

The house was dark, save for a fire in one corner of the kitchen, which softly illuminated the room. A slight woman met them at the door. "You two must be chilled to the bone," she exclaimed as Mario and Rachel entered. "Do come in and warm yourselves by the fire." Meeting Rachel's eyes, she said warmly, "You must be Rachel."

Rachel nodded, again surprised to be known. "And you are—"

"I'm Adara Severus," the woman smiled.

Rachel gasped. The woman she had wanted to find for years!

"I've been good friends with your mother since we were young." Adara seemed to have heard her thoughts. Her smile reached her eyes as she studied Rachel. "In fact, you look much like she did at your age. Wait here; I'll see if she's awake."

Left alone with Mario, Rachel looked at him hard. "What's going on here?" she demanded. "These people act as if they *knew* we were coming!"

"I had a good idea of what you'd want to do when you found out your mother is still alive," he answered quietly. "They said they would be ready if we came. They hold your parents in the highest regard, Rachel."

Mario turned toward Adara, who was walking into the kitchen. "How is she feeling?"

"As well as can be expected. She has a lot of pain, but she's still alert." She placed a hand on Rachel's shoulder. "Your mother is eager to see you," she said softly. "Come with me."

Apprehension knotted Rachel's stomach as she followed Adara down the hall. The chamber they entered was lit only by the moon shining through the window. Adara led the way toward the bed and held up her candle. A woman lay there, her pain-filled face pale against the white pillow under her head. Through the cuts on her face, her eyes shone with something deeper than pain as they met Rachel's.

Rachel caught her breath. The beauty that had radiated from this woman in the arena was still evident. Her mother extended one hand, her gaze clinging to Rachel's face with fierce intensity. "You came," she whispered. "My little Rachel."

Only then did Rachel realize that her mother's cheeks were wet with tears.

Pardon's Price

CHAPTER SIX

O h, my daughter, I thought I would never see you again." Elisabetta's hand trembled as she clasped Rachel's hand in hers. Her voice was thick with tears as she spoke again. "I guess you aren't little Rachel anymore. I left behind a baby, and now you come to me a young woman." Her gaze roamed over Rachel's features as she smiled tremulously. "Adara told me that you look much like I did at your age. But you do look like your father too, that's certain. Did your grandfather consent to letting you come after all?"

Rachel shook her head slowly. "I'm sorry he was so cruel to you, Mother. I found out what happened between the two of you from my slave girl, and I decided to come on my own. I didn't consider the consequences; it was something I had to do."

Her mother squeezed her hand. "The Lord has been with you, dear, or else you wouldn't be here. But tell me about yourself. I want to know everything about my daughter."

Rachel told her mother about life in the grand villa, of her close friendship with Diana, and of how her needs had been met. Not wanting to worry her mother, she left out the details of how angry she had been when she had found out about her grandparents' deception. "I think my grandparents want the best for me," she said with some difficulty.

"I'm certain they do." Her mother's eyes shadowed, and Rachel glimpsed deep pain in them. "But if your grandfather finds out that you're here tonight, he may be angry."

"I am hoping he won't find out," Rachel answered steadily. "I want to be back by morning."

"Then we have to talk fast." Her mother drew a long breath. "Rachel, I want to tell you the story of what happened to separate us from each other those long years ago. Or have you heard it already?"

Rachel shook her head. "My grandparents have never spoken of it to me. All I know is what my friend Bernice told me, back when I was fourteen."

Her mother's eyes widened. "A friend told you?"

"It actually started even before that." Rachel clasped her hands together and leaned forward slightly. "Right around the time I was twelve years old." She told the story of the girl she had found crying beside the lake, and of the baby who would never know her mother. "When I talked to my grandparents about it, they reacted so strangely. I could tell my experience disturbed them. That was the first I had an inkling that something was wrong. But I didn't find out why until Bernice told me."

Elisabetta's grip on Rachel's hand tightened. "Who is Bernice?"

"Rufus and Melora's daughter," Rachel answered.

Tears were misting Elisabetta's eyes now, and a faint smile trembled on her lips. "Rufus and Melora Petronius," she murmured, taking a deep breath. "It's been a long time."

"Bernice told me that you were close to her mother as a girl," Rachel explained softly.

The faint smile grew brighter. "Melora, Adara, and I were inseparable. So Melora's daughter is your friend?"

"Yes, and a good one." Rachel smiled. "Her mother has spoken of your childhood together. It's because of her that I know a little bit about you."

"It sounds just like her. Melora was always tenderhearted." Elisabetta paused and searched her daughter's face. "Has she told you the story of how your father and I disappeared?"

Rachel hesitated. It would never do to tell her mother about the rumors that had spread like wildfire at the time—those repugnant rumors of how her parents had fled capture or ridicule, and of how she had remained behind. Most likely they weren't true at all. She shrugged slightly. "I never heard the whole story."

Elisabetta took a deep breath. "I want to tell you the story from the beginning, Rachel. I grew up as the only child of Julian and Cornelia and was well acquainted with wealth and pleasure. Even then your grandfather served as a senator in the Roman Empire." She paused. "Do you have the bedchamber on the second story of the house, down with the south view?" At Rachel's nod she smiled.

"That was my room too. I used to love sitting on the

balcony morning and evening to let the peace of nature around me soothe my spirit." Her smile widened. "I went there a lot for that purpose after I met your father. He stirred feelings within me that I had never felt before. I was sixteen at the time.

"Marcellus was eighteen when we met, and he had come to Rome from the hills of Laodicea to join the Roman army. Your grandfather worked closely with him and often invited him home to the *cena* in the evening. He never talked much about himself in those times; only enough that we knew his mother had died when he was eight, and his father had remarried three years later. During those three years, his grandmother moved into their home and helped to care for the children—there were four in all. Marcellus was the oldest in his family." Elisabetta grimaced as a stab of pain shot through her body, and Rachel reached out to take her hand. Finally she continued, focusing hard on the words she wanted to say.

"With me he shared more. His mother's death had been hard on him, and he had never been able to accept his father's second marriage and the changes it brought. From then on, he dreamed only of leaving to escape the bitter memories and the situation he found himself in. He felt that he was starting over with his life here in Rome." Elisabetta paused, taking in a slow breath.

"I never questioned him; in my eyes he could do nothing wrong. He proved himself worthy of honor and high esteem in the army; the Emperor appointed him as a legate. Your grandfather did not hesitate in giving his consent to our marriage. We moved to a little cottage about a half mile away from my home villa, and though the army took my new husband away a lot, we were blissfully happy.

"Especially when you came." A smile played around Elisabetta's lips. "Oh, Rachel, how we loved you! Your father wanted to name you after his grandmother Rachel. She had been a bright spot in his childhood and remained close to him through the years. She was part Jewish, but she was far enough removed from her heritage that she had completely left the faith of her fathers.

"You were always a good baby, Rachel. We seldom had trouble with you. Your grandparents visited quite often. We were all proud of you."

She paused there, and Rachel waited quietly. These memories were no doubt bittersweet, and Rachel did not want to interrupt her mother's reverie. At length Elisabetta stirred, and a tear slid down her cheek.

"You were around six months old when things started changing. For weeks I silently observed your father and became sure that something was wrong. One night I questioned him about it and discovered that he was harboring deep anger and bitterness that stemmed from his mother's death. Only now it was spilling out because, after serving four years as legate in the army, the position he'd hoped to be promoted to as governor over our province had been given to another man.

"He had been sure the gods were smiling on him, and he couldn't understand why this happened. His anger deepened and spread as he thought back over his life. He became certain that the gods had singled him out as a doomed man.

"His depression grew worse as the months passed, plunging our marriage into chaos. I was desperate. I pleaded with the gods to restore our happiness—to help me know what to do for him. But there was no answer. Your father laughed at me; he was sure the gods weren't even real." Elisabetta paused and gazed into Rachel's eyes. "I felt helpless. We told no one what was going on, because Marcellus forbade it. There seemed to be no way out, and I found myself agreeing with your father. I hated the gods, and I was also beginning to hate life itself. If it hadn't been for you, I don't know how I would have kept going."

Elisabetta drew a long, shaky breath. More tears were threatening to spill over now, but she held them back and went on. "Your father was at the point where he thought death was the only way out. Then one night a stranger knocked on our door just as we were sitting down to supper. As he came into the room, his presence immediately cheered the place. He said he had come from a long distance away and needed a place to stay for the night. It was plain to see; his garments were trail-worn and dusty. Your father invited him to sit down at the table with us.

"To this day, I'm not sure how the man managed to draw out your father. I had hardly been able to get Marcellus to talk to me anymore. He listened patiently to what your father had to say and then explained to us something I will never forget."

She smiled at Rachel and squeezed her hand. "He told us the way of truth. The way of Jesus Christ, the Son of God, who died as a sacrifice for our sins and rose again to give us eternal life. He told us that his God can forgive our sins and release us from the desire to sin. He also spoke of the joy found in experiencing a relationship with this living God. He gave us a copy of some of the writings of the apostle John. Before he left that night, both your father and I chose to worship this God, believing that He was the only true God.

"Of course, we realized the danger ahead. But we believed that the living God would help us. We also knew that when we died, we would live forever with God in a beautiful, perfect place called heaven. We knew that our suffering would end when we died. No amount of torture on earth can separate us from God after death.

"Your father resigned from the army, knowing that he could no longer persecute Christians. In doing so, he had to explain his reasoning, and this put us in a dangerous position. Your father was jailed for a few weeks to be questioned by both the Emperor and his father-in-law. Many friends tried to reason with him—and with me too. Adara and Melora proved to be true friends during this time.

"Your father was finally released, allowed to return home with the condition that he would think things through and change his mind. He was to appear before the jury within a week. We immediately began making plans to escape. We knew we had to be gone by the time that week was up. We wanted to go to the country, thinking that we would find safety there.

"One night before the week was over, we planned to attend a meeting the Christians were holding in the woods not too far from our house. Your grandmother visited us that afternoon. You were so happy—cooing, kicking, smiling. She offered to take you home for the evening. Your grandparents used to do that, just take you home to enjoy you while Marcellus and I spent the evening doing something else, though they hadn't since we'd become Christians. I was thankful for what I thought seemed a softening of their hearts toward our new way of life; then too, it was cold that night, and I'd been worrying about how you were going to handle it. I didn't think anything else was going on."

Elisabetta lifted her eyes, and Rachel flinched at the pain there. "That night at the meeting, persecutors found us. Your grandfather had discovered the plans for the meeting and ordered out a search party. Your father and I both escaped, but we knew it wasn't wise to go back. Even so, I told Marcellus I must go back. My baby was in the hands of people who had known what would happen to us and had deliberately taken her from us. I didn't think I would ever be able to forgive myself if I didn't try to get you back, but your father wouldn't allow it. He said I'd be walking into sure death if I went back; Father had already been heartless enough to send out a search party for the Christians who had escaped. He had been grieved about our decision from the beginning. He tried to convince us to give up our faith, and your grandmother shed many tears over the matter.

"When he saw that all his persuasion was useless, Father became very angry. It seemed as though his pride awakened and took hold of him. He had shouted at Marcellus the last time they were together that we'd be sorry for this step we had taken. He said he would see to it that he destroyed our faith before it advanced any further. We hadn't known what he meant to do, but his intentions became painfully clear.

"My parents' betrayal and the experience of losing you didn't destroy our faith, but we came close to giving up. It was a long time before I was finally able to leave you in God's hands and trust Him to work everything out for good. Your father struggled with it, too. Daily we reminded each other that God was with you and would take care of you.

"And you know what?" Elisabetta waited until Rachel met her gaze. "I still believe God will work out something good from those experiences."

"How can you believe that?" Rachel whispered.

"We know that all things work together for good to those who love God," her mother answered softly. "It says that in the Scriptures. Because I love God and believe in His love for me, He will work out something good from what seems impossibly bad. God delights in blessing His children. It's His marvelous ways that have led our paths together tonight. Can you not feel that?"

Rachel looked down, not sure how to answer. When she lifted her head, her eyes were misty with tears. "I've watched many people die in the arena at the Colosseum, Mother. It's not hard to see that Christians meet death differently from the gladiators and criminals. I haven't really believed in the gods for a long time. And if they're real, they're not kind and they don't seem to give anything to their subjects unless they're bribed. They don't offer a reason to live. My life seems purposeless.

"Oh, there are things that bring me happiness—my friends make life interesting enough. But the future appears as dark as midnight. No one is able to tell me the answers; no one knows. And—" Rachel stopped, collecting her thoughts.

"And?" Elisabetta asked quietly.

"That's when I think of the Christians. I have watched many people die in the arena. The prisoners die in an agony of fear, crying out to their gods for deliverance. The Christians die peacefully, even joyfully. Sometimes they sing. Other times . . ." Her voice trailed away, and she looked at her mother, a mute appeal in her eyes. "Men shout words to the throngs, like my father did. Their words always indicate that they are going somewhere—a place of glory. But for the gladiators and criminals, there seems to be no hope."

"I can see that you have been thinking hard about this already," Elisabetta acknowledged softly.

"As a child, I had a real terror of the Colosseum," Rachel went on. "I always wanted to hold up my thumbs to the men pleading for mercy. I cried when the thumbs all around me went down. Grandfather often tried to tell me that those men did not need mercy. To him, they were only common slaves—criminals who deserved death—but to me they were people.

"When the Christians began entering the arena, their courage amazed me. I've heard much about your people, Mother, such as how they refuse to worship the gods of Rome. The Emperor is afraid that the gods are angry. He is certain the Christians plot to destroy the Empire, and that is why he is determined to destroy them. But these are rumors I have never believed, especially when I watch the Christians die in the arena. They are too peaceable to be dangerous."

She stopped, her eyes intense as they searched her mother's. "Death never fills the Christians with fear—at least, it doesn't seem to. How can this be?"

Mother placed one hand over her heart. "The thought of death brings natural fear, Rachel. That's only human. But when we walked into the arena, I was not afraid. Deep in my heart I knew I was ready to die."

"Knew—how?" Rachel whispered hoarsely.

"Jesus said, 'Take up your cross and follow me.' That's what your father and I did—took up the cross of pain, danger, trials, whatever life brought our way—and we followed Jesus," Elisabetta answered simply. "It brought death to your father yesterday. Whether or not taking up the cross will require physical death, it will require death to self. It means surrendering to God's will for our lives and living daily for Him. It also means salvation and eternal life in glory."

"Heaven—what do you think it is?" Rachel asked.

"Everyone goes somewhere after they die," Elisabetta explained. "As Christians, we know we have a home with God where we will go after death. He told us so. 'In my Father's house are many mansions . . . I go to prepare a place for you.' Our time here on earth is just a short journey that we must each take to get there. After we die, time is no more. We enter eternity."

"And those who aren't Christians?" As she spoke, Rachel tensed. "Those men who die in the arena—they have no hope. They die in agonizing fear. Where do they go?"

Her mother hesitated. "God is the judge of all men," she said slowly. "We can know that these men are in His hands, wherever they are. The Scriptures tell of a place where the ungodly go—a place called hell. It's a place where everything is burning all the time. Rachel, the devil is an evil being, desperately trying to turn people away from truth. He hates God and is doing his best to destroy God's followers. That's why so many are dying. The devil hates the way Christianity is spreading."

"Who is God?" Rachel asked. "Diana said that you believe your God is real, and that He answers your prayers. I have yet to see a god who will answer all the prayers poured out to him!"

Elisabetta's eyes lit up. "Do you ever wonder who created the earth around you? We are brought up believing it was the gods; but don't you think it was a Being much more wise and powerful than any other god?"

"I don't believe in any of the gods, Mother."

"But wait until I tell you about my God!" Elisabetta smiled. "There is joy in living for Him, because He is a loving God. He has never been born and will never die. He always existed and will exist forever. He cares about each of His children, and we only need to trust and follow His leading. And when the time comes for us to die, He takes us to glory to live with Him.

"He asks only that you give your all to Him, Rachel, and to believe His gift of salvation. He came down to earth as a baby and grew up as a human. He taught people the way of truth. He came to die to take the punishment for our sins! We may try to do good, but of ourselves we are nothing. Jesus died on a cross as a sacrifice that satisfied God's punishment for sin. God says we don't ever need to offer another sacrifice again. We only need to trust in Jesus' perfect sacrifice. It's a gift for everyone who will believe Him."

"But—to commit my whole life to this God?" Rachel whispered, barely able to breathe.

"Yes! To use as He chooses," her mother replied softly. "He has a special plan for you, Rachel, and all you have to do is ask for His gift of salvation. Your sins will be forgiven, and you can make a fresh start with your life."

"I want peace," Rachel said earnestly. "My life is full of turmoil, and I feel so much hatred for people who've done horrible things. It makes me feel all tight and dark inside.

I don't think it's possible for me, though, to ask this God to take control of my life. It requires too much."

"It is a high price, Rachel," her mother answered. "But this giving of your whole self to God is worth the choice. You will find peace, and you'll find the supernatural ability to pardon others. I faced the temptation to let hatred toward your grandfather take control of me. But by God's grace, I was able to forgive him."

"I can't understand it," Rachel murmured. "How can you forgive your father for what he did to you?"

"God loves me and is willing to forgive my sins—sins that are just as bad as anything your grandfather ever did," Elisabetta answered gently. "How can I do less than to forgive those who wrong me? Wouldn't you like to forgive him yourself, Rachel?"

It sounds so easy. But even as the thought flashed through Rachel's mind, all the anger that she had felt toward her grandfather swelled into a great tide that rushed through her whole being. She pressed her lips together in anger. Forgive? "I'll never forgive that man for what he has done to our family." The thought spilled through her mouth before she could restrain it.

"Then you're right back where you started, Rachel." The soft words were laced with sadness. "But there is something I want you to do. Reach under my bed, please, and pull out the parchments you find there."

Puzzled, Rachel knelt down. She picked up pages of animal-skin parchment folded together in a makeshift book form. "Some of those are copies of letters that the apostle Paul wrote to the Romans about two hundred years ago," her mother was saying, her voice tinged with awe. "Other pages are copies of the Gospel written by the apostle John. And then there are several pages of psalms written by the ancient Jewish king, David."

Rachel's eyes grew large as she fingered the carefully handwritten pages. "And these are yours?" she asked. Her grandfather owned numerous books because he was wealthy, but very few of the common people had the means to own even one book.

"Yes, they are," her mother said, smiling through her pain. "Your father and I were very blessed to receive our own copy of these letters. They are God's Word to mankind. What you read in those pages will show you the way to forgiveness better than I ever can, and they'll also show you the way of the cross that God wants His people to carry. Take it home with you when you leave and read it for yourself. Will you promise me this?"

"I can't promise I'll become a Christian," countered Rachel quietly.

"I'm not asking you to do that." Elisabetta looked deeply into her eyes. "I just want you to read these words. I'm giving them to you. I'm not going to live much longer."

Tears welled up in Rachel's eyes as she stroked the rough parchment. "Oh, Mother. I wish—" As her throat choked up, she turned away.

Mother squeezed her hand gently. "Remember, daughter," she whispered. "My prayers will follow you all through your life. And God will follow you all your life too. He'll never give up knocking at your heart's door. I pray that you will one day be able to know the fulfillment of life that comes from serving Him. And then we will meet again."

CHAPTER SEVEN

When Mario and Rachel rode out of the horse stables together, the sky was a deep violet-blue hue, with faint streaks of rose and lavender painting the eastern horizon. Only once did Rachel look back to glimpse the light from a window of the villa as they paused at a bend in the road. "Goodbye, Mother," she whispered, fighting back the lump in her throat.

She slipped one hand inside the folds of her garment and let her fingers gently touch her mother's parchments. *I will read it*, she promised herself silently. *I'll read it and find out how the Christian can face death so joyfully. But the way of the cross sounds too—*

"Rachel?" Mario spoke softly as he reined in his horse beside her. "Your mother is a heroic woman."

Rachel's heart warmed at his statement. "I'm not at all sorry I came," she replied, taking a deep breath. "Even though we're most likely going to get home late enough that my grandparents will question where I was, every minute of it was worthwhile." She pulled the parchments from her cloak, her eyes shining with unshed tears as she studied the pages in the breaking dawn. "This was my mother's gift to me. It was hers, and now it's mine."

"Did she tell you anything about your family?" Mario spurred his horse into a trot, leading the way around the bend into the forest.

"I have two sisters and three brothers," answered Rachel. "Alexandros is only a year younger than I. Then it's Katerina, fourteen—Makarios, eleven—Hadrianus, eight—and Melodia, seven. When he was a baby, Hadrianus was left an orphan after both of his parents died, and my parents took him as their own." She paused, intensity gleaming in her black eyes. "Someday I will find them, if it's the last thing I do. Just think of it, Mario! They are my brothers and sisters!"

"Did your mother say where they're living?"

"She said they've been living down in the catacombs. Because my father was one of their leaders, it wasn't safe for him to remain above ground. My parents were captured when they came up with some other Christians to visit a sick man on his deathbed."

"I've heard a little about the catacombs," Mario said thoughtfully. "They're extensive, aren't they?"

"There are numerous passages, I know that much. And it's dark down there, a place where they bury their dead." Rachel shivered slightly, her tone lowering. "I hate to think of going somewhere like that. But if my family lives there, I want to see them. I can't imagine living in the catacombs for a long time, like they have. How they keep up their courage and faith, I simply can't figure out."

"They have strong beliefs," Mario answered speculatively. "Perhaps those writings your mother gave you will answer some of your questions about their faith."

"She already explained it to me." For a moment Rachel studied the parchments, and then slipped them within the folds of her garment. "I understand the Christians better now. But I want to read it all for myself in these pages."

"The Christian faith sounds so difficult."

The words hung between them in the still air for a long moment. Then Rachel answered quietly, "More than you know."

"How true that is, journal. How could my parents find it in their hearts to forgive my grandfather? Accepting the gift of salvation from the God these Christians serve sounds too easy—but the way of the cross sounds too hard."

Rachel lifted her head, allowing the cool breeze to soothe the hot flush in her cheeks as she thought over the words she had just written. "I am not going to the Colosseum today," she said aloud, taking a deep breath. "I have attended for the last time. No one is dragging me there again."

"No one is dragging you where?"

Rachel jumped and whirled around. Her grandfather stood in the doorway of her chamber, looking through the room to where Rachel sat on her balcony. Rachel's fingers fumbled as she hastily rolled up the scroll and stood up.

"Just talking to myself," she said lightly, leaning over the railing. "It's gorgeous out here, isn't it?"

She didn't miss the relief that flashed through her grandfather's eyes as he moved toward her. "I think these days are beginning to show their strain on all of us," he said with a faint smile.

Rachel kept her gaze on the sky, not daring to meet her grandfather's eyes lest he see the truth there—the reality that she had not slept at all the night before. Her eyelids felt heavy, and she had noticed violet shadows under her eyes when she had glanced briefly at her reflection. It would never do to let her grandparents see her fatigue, lest they suspect anything about her night's escapade.

"I didn't sleep well last night," Julian admitted, joining Rachel at the railing. "I'm worried about your mother. Last night her heart took a turn for the worse." He paused, his brow furrowing into a troubled frown. "I want you to come down and sit with her."

"Why did she faint the other day at the Colosseum, Father?" Rachel glanced at him sideways. As the wind caught his once-black hair, Rachel noticed more streaks of gray than she remembered. In the morning sunlight, his face looked old. For a moment, unbidden pity touched her heart. Then she stiffened. *He's worried about his wife? Well, he deserves it.*

"I suppose everything got to be too much for her, that's all. I know these days have been wearing me down." He turned away and then glanced back. "As soon as you're ready."

"I'll hurry," Rachel promised, stepping into the chamber. She halted before her dressing table and stared at the girl in the glass. She had planned to wear her turquoise silk tunic today—the deep blue color was her favorite, reminding her of peaceful early mornings and late twilights she so often watched from her balcony. Her friends had told her it was the color that became her most, setting off her black hair and eyes. But now she changed her mind, choosing a pale green linen tunic instead. The turquoise silk would be in open controversy with her feelings if she wore it.

When Rachel entered her grandmother's chamber, Cornelia was lying still and silent in bed, her delicate features and lips taut even in sleep. Rachel stood looking down at her, studying the familiar face carefully. The pain had left its imprint, and in that imprint Rachel could see an anguish that went deeper than physical pain. On impulse, she reached out and placed her hand over the wrinkled one. "It's a miracle you're still alive," she whispered. "How much more can your heart take?"

There was no answer. Her grandmother's chest rose and fell with each breath that came, growing slower and slower. Rachel squeezed the slim hand slightly, alarmed now. "Mother? Mother, wake up!"

But instead of waking, Cornelia began to moan and toss in her sleep, her forehead damp with sweat. *Must be a nightmare,* Rachel thought. *She certainly isn't waking up. I wonder what's going through her mind right now— scenes from yesterday or from long years ago?* Standing up, Rachel paced restlessly toward the window, where she looked out into the peristyle gardens. *What part did my grandmother play in all this, anyway? She tried to reason with my parents to give up their faith, that much I know. But does she know that her husband went to visit their daughter yesterday morning?* Rachel doubted it.

With a cry her grandmother awoke, struggling to sit up in bed. "What's going on here?" she asked huskily, staring at Rachel as she moved toward the bed.

"Lie down again, Mother," Rachel said softly, placing

both hands on her shoulders and pushing her gently backward. "You had a heart spell, remember? You must be careful."

"Yes, I must be careful." Cornelia sighed deeply and rested her head against the pillow, her gaze vacant as she watched Rachel. "Do you know what happened in the arena yesterday?"

"I do." Rachel tucked the blankets more closely around her and stroked the salt-and-pepper hair that fell across the sunken cheeks.

Cornelia struggled up on one elbow, her eyes terrified now. "But you shouldn't have seen it!" she cried.

"Calm down, Mother." Rachel pushed her back again. "You shouldn't talk now. Just relax and try to rest, okay?"

Cornelia sank back against the bed, her eyes drifting shut. "Rest," she murmured. "What is rest? I will never . . ." She stirred uncomfortably and then fell silent.

Relieved, Rachel waited until her grandmother was once again breathing the even breath of sleep before she slipped out of the room. *No one wants to tell me what's going on. I'd go crazy if I didn't already know. Father is destroying the whole family over this.*

Forgiveness. That mystery word kept returning to her thoughts. Such a strange principle to uphold in a world torn by hatred, strife, greed, and cruelty. She couldn't begin to understand it.

Although Rachel would rather have remained at home to reflect on the events of the night before, she responded immediately to the servant girl's message that Athena was asking for her. As she neared the large villa, however, Rachel found her steps lagging. How could she be a help to Athena when her own heart was in such turmoil?

A servant led Rachel to her friend's room, where she found Athena sitting in a chair, looking pale. "How are you, Athena?" Rachel asked.

Athena looked at Rachel with hollow eyes.

"I'm never going back to the Colosseum." A shudder coursed through her frame. "There is nothing glorious about it."

"How are you going to tell your parents that?" Rachel asked quietly.

Athena shrugged her shoulders. "They'll just have to understand." She took a deep breath. "Rachel, it's such a cruel world. Going to the Colosseum makes you lose your heart and become calloused to death and violence. Those that attend are bloodthirsty vampires—all of them. It takes away your loved ones. You lose all the sanity you once had. Family ties are severed, and people begin to think like the murderers they are until you're no longer safer in your own home." Her dark eyes flashed as she sat up. "Like Emperor Nero. He killed his mother—he even took his own life and—"

"Athena, calm down!" Rachel caught her friend's shoulders, alarmed. The girl was breathing hard, her eyes slightly glazed. Finally Athena took a deep breath and exhaled slowly.

"I'm sorry, Rachel," she murmured, sinking her head into the pillow again. "I just get so angry—Cadmus's death replays in my mind and haunts my dreams. I don't understand why I ever enjoyed the Colosseum. Now I hate it with a deadly hatred."

Rachel squeezed her hand. "I'm sorry, Athena. If I could have, I would've jumped into the arena and saved Cadmus myself."

"That's what hurt the most." Athena's eyes drifted shut. "To watch him die, unable to do anything about it. I watch it over and over in my dreams."

"You do have the memory of his love for you," Rachel said quietly.

Athena made an impatient movement with her head against the pillow. "Memories are not enough, Rachel. I'll never see him again." Silent tears were trembling on her eyelashes now.

Rachel swallowed hard and stepped back, knowing there was nothing more she could do for the girl before her. She thought of her mother, whom she would probably never see again. But she knew that now was not the time to tell Athena the story. She stayed with Athena for a while, making small talk to try to take her friend's mind off her troubles. Her heart grieved at the distress she saw resting on the girl's strong features.

Finally she said, "Athena, just remember that I'm thinking about you, and I care."

"Thanks, Rachel." Athena smiled faintly. "You're a true friend."

Troubled at heart, Rachel escaped from the room, making no effort to slow her steps as she hurried down the stairs. Tears stung her own eyes as she walked down the sunlit streets. The streets were nearly deserted at this hour, a sign that everyone was attending the Circus Maximus.

Throwing back her *palla*, Rachel let the wind play with her hair as she lifted her face toward the sky. Perhaps she could go to the sea. No doubt this wind was whipping up high waves that foamed with a salty mist. She loved the sea when it was in that mood. Besides, she wanted to be alone, and the sea was ideal for that.

With anticipation, she quickly turned in the direction of the sea, nearly crashing into someone behind her. With a startled gasp she stepped back. "I'm sorry! I didn't know anyone was around," she exclaimed, the heat rushing into her face.

The young man's smile was warm, amusement twitching the corners of his mouth. "It's my fault more than yours. I just stepped out of my shop—I should have let you know I was behind you."

Rachel surveyed the man. He looked to be in his mid-twenties, with curly black hair that seemed to match the twinkling humor in his eyes. They sobered as he returned her gaze. "You are Rachel Gallus, aren't you?"

"Ah . . . I—" Rachel paused, suddenly wary.

The young man spared her from answering. "I have a message for you from Adara Severus," he said quietly, and Rachel snapped to attention. Rather than explaining himself immediately, he opened the shop door behind them and stepped inside. "Why don't you come in here? No one seems to be around, but I don't want to take any chances."

Rachel cautiously followed him into the cool, dark interior of the shop. He appeared to be a pottery merchant, displaying beautiful vessels on the surrounding shelves. She liked the place at once.

He stepped behind the counter and turned to face her. "I understand you went to see your mother during the night," he began. "Adara said that she took a turn for the worse after you were gone, and the physician does not expect her to live too much longer. Here—" Bending lower, he reached into the shelves beneath the counter and returned with a piece of papyrus in one hand. "You are to give this to Melora Petronius. Don't let anyone know it's in your possession."

"A message?" Rachel gave it a quick glance as she took it from him. She saw the words, "A farewell message to Melora from Elisabetta herself."

"How do you know Adara Severus?" she asked softly.

He hesitated a moment, as though weighing his words carefully before he answered. "They are raising my little daughter. My wife died four years ago, leaving me with a tiny baby. I couldn't take care of her on my own, so I gave her to Adara and her husband Simon, who are trustworthy people. They agreed to raise Aquilina as their own. I visit the family every now and then."

"I see. I didn't meet much of the family while I was there."

His brief smile revealed sadness. "My daughter is in good hands. I thank God for His divine leading in our lives."

She gazed at him keenly. "You are a Christian?"

"Since I met Simon and Adara," he confirmed. "God has been good to us."

He nodded toward the paper. "Take it to Melora Petronius, as I said. Remember, no one must know that you're delivering it."

Rachel nodded solemnly. "I'll be careful," she promised, opening the door.

"Of that I have no doubt. And I will keep you informed about your mother," he answered, walking out from behind the counter.

On the sidewalk she paused and turned back. "I don't believe I discovered your name."

His grin flashed in the sunlight, his dark eyes twinkling again. "Philip Lucius, at your service," he said with a slight bow. "Go—and God be with you."

PARDON'S PRICE

CHAPTER EIGHT

The *cena* was as quiet a meal as Rachel remembered ever attending. The silence so heavy it could almost be felt.

She exchanged a wordless glance with Diana as the girl placed a tray of apricots on the table. On the other side where he reclined on his couch, her grandfather did not look up. He seemed lost in his own world, staring absently out the window, his heavy brows furrowed. Even the loud crash of a breaking platter, dropped by a nervous young servant as he came through the door with both arms laden, did not make him stir.

"I'm sorry," Jovan whispered, sounding close to tears as he stared at the floor. Figs rolled everywhere, thumping across the rugs and breaking the stillness of the room. Rachel felt herself relaxing.

"There's no need to fret," she said kindly, rising from her couch. She wasn't hungry—and with such a silent meal as this, she would rather be elsewhere, anyway. "Diana, will you help clean it up? Father, I believe I will excuse myself."

"Wait." Her grandfather straightened abruptly, his gaze suddenly piercing as he called after her. Rachel, already halfway to the door, halted in mid-step and glanced back in surprise. Her grandfather hadn't spoken a word to her all throughout the meal. Why would he now?

Turning, she moved toward the window and waited, glancing involuntarily at the beckoning twilight filtering through the panes. She squelched a sudden impulse to fling back the curtain and flee through the window. Whatever her grandfather had to say, she was not interested in hearing it.

"I asked Justin to join us tonight," Father said, his hand unsteady as he reached for the wine glass Jovan had set before him. "But he had a court trial to attend. It seems they have caught more Christians."

Rachel took a deep breath. *If that's all he wants with me—*

But her grandfather continued. "If you would be a man, I would ask you to attend one of these trials and see for yourself what goes on, Rachel. I do hope you are not getting the idea that these Christians are right in what they're doing. They deserve to be punished. And I certainly hope you will never let yourself be sucked into their system of teachings and practices. I'll do everything in my power to keep you from that."

He paused and drummed his fingers rhythmically against the table. "It seems that we are getting somewhere with this, though. Earlier this week, one of their leaders was killed in the arena. Last night Fabian and Justin brought in two Christian men. One of them is—was—one of the leaders of the church. If we find all the leaders, we will be able to stop these people." A hint of a smile touched Father's lips. "You should be proud of what our soldiers are doing for Rome."

"Why are you telling me this?" Rachel asked quietly.

Julian shot her a quick glance and then spoke simply. "I have arranged your marriage to Fabian, Rachel. I've had my eye on the young man for a long time. He has far exceeded my expectations in this work of capturing Christians—and most of all, he knows where he stands in what he believes."

Rachel, shocked into numbness, had only one thought. *And you don't want to make a mistake with me like you did with my mother—is that it?*

"I know of no other man I would rather see you with than Fabian, Rachel," Julian was saying. "The date for your wedding isn't set yet, but we will celebrate as soon as your mother is able."

He paused, as though waiting for a response. Rachel turned slowly to face him, composed and cool. "May I be excused now, Father?"

He studied her closely for a moment and nodded. "I know this may be a surprise to you. But I want only what's best for you, and I know you will be grateful someday."

Rachel escaped from the room, knowing that if she stayed a moment longer she would lose control. She crashed into Diana as she burst through the kitchen doorway, and another tray fell to the floor, splitting a jug of wine in half. As the crimson liquid traveled slowly across the floor, Rachel felt her stomach heave. *It looks so much like the blood of . . .*

Diana didn't give her time to think about it. "There's

someone here to see you," she said, grabbing Rachel's arm. "He says his name is Philip Lucius."

"Philip Lucius!" Rachel righted herself against the doorjamb and straightened abruptly. Diana was already vanishing into the kitchen, no doubt going back for a cloth to clean up the spilled wine. Turning, Rachel walked down the hall toward the atrium in a daze, feeling as though her world were spinning so fast she could hardly keep up with it.

She led Philip out to the peristyle, where they could speak together privately. Philip wasted no time in getting to the point. "Adara's husband, Simon, is in prison."

Rachel caught her breath. So this was the leader her father was referring to.

Philip went on, lowering his voice. "I talked with Simon an hour or so before his capture. He said your mother passed away early this morning, and they were preparing her body for burial in the catacombs. If you want to come with me—"

"I'm ready," said Rachel immediately.

Philip's tone lowered even more. "We will go to Simon's house and travel with his family into the catacombs. They are planning to move there, since it's not safe for them to remain aboveground any longer."

Rachel was already stepping toward the door. "Tell the stable boy to have a horse ready for me," she said over her shoulder.

Philip nodded. "I'll meet you beyond the city gates."

———————◆◆◆———————

The catacombs were even worse than Rachel had feared. Damp, dark, and cold, the walls closed in around her until she felt her throat clog up and her breath trap itself in her chest. She had always hated darkness and tight dwellings, and this was the essence of her phobias.

"And people actually live down here?" she asked.

"Scores of them," came the answer. Turning, Philip lifted his torch higher, searching her face by the light that fell across it. "This is what they live with all the time."

Rachel shuddered. They had been traveling for an hour or so now, and the only people she had seen were her companions—the Severus family, Philip, and his daughter. Petite Aquilina was sleeping on her father's shoulder, her golden brown curls gleaming in the light of the torch.

"See there?" Philip halted and shone the torch downward, lighting up the path at their feet. "It is an opening that leads below. There are many passages below even that. These catacombs cover a span of many miles."

Rachel stared into what appeared to be a bottomless pit, and another shudder coursed through her. "A few years ago you would not have been able to persuade me to come here," she said quietly. "I know these catacombs are sacred burial grounds, but they are smothering and oppressive. You could get lost and never find your way out again."

"Which is why the soldiers are afraid to come and search out the Christians." Adara Severus spoke softly, gesturing toward the left. "See how this path intersects with another? That's how it is the whole way through. The fossors—those who dig out the graves and excavate sand for building cement—have sometimes led soldiers through these paths until their torches run out. Then the soldiers ask to be led back, and nothing ever comes of their search."

"No wonder they ask to be led back," Rachel murmured. "If I'd have to walk in nothing but this darkness, I'd go crazy."

"Most of these fossors are Christians themselves," Philip said. "They will not betray their fellow men."

She gave him a troubled glance. "You are so loyal to each other. In my society, I can hardly trust anyone. My own grandfather—" She stopped abruptly.

"Christ's love is loyal," answered Philip softly. "As we become His children, He ties us together with a bond of love that is loyal and true to one another. It's a love greater than any other love found on earth," he added. "And if you seek it, you'll find it."

Silence reigned as they walked on. Sometimes they stooped, ducking under the ceiling as it sloped downward. At other times the path widened, lessening the claustrophobic sensation. As Rachel grew accustomed to the darkness, her gloom lifted. Down here, it seemed as though no other world existed. The burdens weighing on her mind faded in significance and left the door open to other matters of interest.

Like the tablets along the wall, appearing with inscriptions written on them, marking a tomb. Rachel caught only a brief glimpse of those inscriptions as she passed by, but enough to notice the word occurring most: *Peace. Is it really possible to die in peace? What does that mean? Oh, God . . . if you're there—*

The faint, faraway melody of song broke into the tentative thought. Rachel listened intently. Pausing, Adara placed a hand on her shoulder. "The Christians have gathered for the burial. They are singing now."

Rachel nodded and moved forward, the melody becoming louder and clearer with every step she took. It was unlike anything she had ever heard before, carrying a strain of beauty that took on a divine tone. They were singing about God dwelling with men, and about the end of death and sorrow and pain. "It's breathtaking," Rachel whispered as the song ended. There was a Presence here. She felt as if she were standing on hallowed ground.

A gentle pressure on her arm told her that it was time to move on. Taking a deep breath, she squared her shoulders and followed Philip and Adara until they came in view of the circle of singers.

———————◆◆◆◆◆———————

Rachel could never forget the last view of her mother. There she lay, ashen pale in death, yet with a faint smile still on her lips as though she had passed away peacefully. Rachel bent over the casket, silent tears falling down her cheeks. *Oh, Mother,* her broken heart cried. *I'd give anything to erase the past and really be your daughter!*

She thought of her father. The tall man had stood firmly straight like an oak tree in the arena, his voice a booming command of authority that hushed the crowds and awakened the sense of change within her heart. Were her parents even now in that place they called heaven?

The others were stirring all around her, making way for a group of young men moving forward. Rachel stepped back, watching silently as they passed. Most likely they had been chosen to carry the stone sarcophagus to the niche in the wall where it would rest. A tall young man at the front of the small procession caught her eye. He walked with a purposeful bearing, just like—she caught her breath. Could this be Alexandros, the fifteen-year-old brother her mother had spoken about?

As the people gathered around the tomb, Rachel remained next to the wall, struck by the expressions engraved in those faces. There was sorrow, yes; but the quiet joy and peace from deep within seemed to pervade the whole atmosphere, as though there were something beyond the finality of the grave to bring hope and comfort to their aching hearts.

The words of the speaker clarified this as he spoke from where he stood before the tomb. "A dear sister has left us and gone on to her eternal reward. We grieve the loss and we cry for the perilous times in which we live. But we can rest knowing that she is with the Lord, and happier there than she could ever be here. She knows no sorrow or pain."

Rachel couldn't help thinking of the burials she was accustomed to. Death was such a fearsome thing. Here it merely portrayed the passing of a soul into a glorious eternity, a death that brought joy in the midst of sorrow. She had often witnessed that same kind of joy in the arena. Could she ever know it as her own? She glanced sideways to find that Adara had moved up beside her, holding Aquilina in her arms. This lady's husband was in prison even now, awaiting an almost sure sentence of death. How could she be so calm? Or was she hiding feelings that would erupt like a violent storm if unleashed?

How did her own siblings feel? She had already picked them out—the small group standing to the left of the sarcophagus. An elderly couple stood with them, as well as a younger lady she surmised to be the minister's wife. She should be with them, but instead she was here among the crowd, denied her birthright as a sister and daughter because of circumstances that were beyond her control. Why was she the victim of all that hatred and pride?

Just then, she felt Adara's hand on her arm. "Come with me," she whispered. "You need to stand with your own family."

Rachel felt the heat flush her face. Had Adara heard her thoughts? But she was already moving forward. Swallowing hard, Rachel followed. The people were singing again, a chorus that spoke of everlasting life with Jesus. It swelled triumphantly around her, bringing unbidden tears to her eyes. These people truly did believe in their faith—believed with all their hearts.

The sound of thudding boots, shouting men, and clinking armor was heard coming from around the bend in the corridor. The Christians were no longer alone. Flaming torches pierced the semi-darkness, lighting up the towering chamber and seeming to declare that escape was impossible. "Soldiers!" Adara whispered, her eyes widening.

The glittering crimson uniforms gleamed as a dozen or more soldiers rushed through the entrance, brandishing clubs and spears. But the Christians were already disappearing, melting through doorways Rachel had not realized were there. Adara turned to her, urgency in her eyes. "You must not be found here, Rachel. Run!"

But Rachel remained frozen in place, her eyes on a young soldier grabbing a child's arm nearby. As he turned, she swayed, suddenly feeling faint. "Justin!"

As the gasp left her lips, her cousin whirled around. His jaw dropped. "What are you—are my eyes deceiving me?"

She could only shake her head, her dark gaze probing deeply into his. Justin released the child's arm and was at her side in one stride, catching her arm in a vice-like grip as his voice dropped to a low, urgent tone. "There's no time to talk. Whatever you're doing here, it'll have to wait 'til later. Now run—I'll cover for you."

She didn't wait. Turning on her heels, she fled from the chamber and into the corridor.

Blackness. As the light of torches faded, Rachel became aware of a blackness so dense and deep that it seemed as though the evil raging behind her was closing in even here. Observing her cousin in action was a shock. This was what Rome asked of its valiant soldiers?

Rachel felt that the darkness surrounding her had become a symbol of her own past and future.

CHAPTER NINE

> I met my siblings—Katerina, Makarios, Hadrianus, and Melodia. The background of those early years in our family story was no secret to them, and they knew all about me. They accepted me as a sister, freely and unconditionally.

Rachel wrote in her journal, grateful to be on her balcony again. She had been found by the Christians in the dark corridors of the catacombs, and they had helped her find her way out. But although she sat in her familiar spot again, her world was shaken irreparably. Never again would it be what she had always known as normal.

The stylus flowed across the page again.

> But I didn't get to meet Alexandros. The soldiers took him away before I had a chance. I'm worried that I'll have to watch his death as well. Of course, I

could just deny that he's in the Colosseum. I wouldn't have to go find out. But something compels me.

A chill gripped her heart. "Rachel?" Diana's voice broke into her reverie as she stepped out the door onto the balcony. She placed her arm around Rachel's shoulders in wordless sympathy.

"I don't want to go to the arena tomorrow," Rachel said vehemently, "but something deep inside says I must."

Diana's gaze was searching. "Something is changing in your heart, Rachel. What you told me last night when you arrived home from the catacombs makes me think that the Christian faith is influencing you."

Rachel didn't answer for a long moment. Finally she said in a whisper, "You're absolutely right."

"And?" prompted Diana when she didn't go on.

"My family is amazing. I appreciate so much what I see in them. And I want what they have, but I'm not sure I'm willing to pay the price." Her tone lowered to a fierce whisper. "I don't know that I can ever forgive my grandfather for what he has done to all of us."

How was it possible to feel so alone in the midst of a sea of people? Rachel wondered about that as she stood in the corridor of the Colosseum, watching the activity below. The sound of swords clashing in gladiatorial combat, of men screaming in agony, of multitudes applauding—it contrasted sharply with the quiet joy and peace she had experienced in the catacombs with the Christians. Philip had told her that Christ's children were tied together with a bond of love that motivated them to be loyal and true to each other. The kingdom represented here, a dominion of hatred and lust for power, was completely different.

Raw hatred closed its tentacles around the Christians when they filed into the arena. Rachel could sense the evil forces at work among the throngs as she leaned forward, straining to discern the figures.

Human torches, men hung on crosses, were lit up around the arena as fires burned at their bases, creeping up the wood to engulf the prisoners in crackling flames. As the stench of singed hair and flesh filled the air, Rachel caught sight of him—her brother. His eyes were closed, his lips moving. Rachel closed her eyes in horror. Why had he chosen the way of the cross when it meant his own death on a cross? That choice was humanly impossible to make.

Rachel lingered until she could stand it no longer. Then she fled down the flights of stairs to the street, pausing only once to look back. It was then that a picture formed in her mind's eye—a vivid revelation of the raging conflict between two powerful kingdoms, one reigning on earth and the other in heaven. She saw Rome as if it lay in ashes, a great city ruined by mankind's greed and tyranny. The acrid scent of smoke filled its streets, and thousands of voices wailed as their souls fell into the pits of hell. *And here I stand, alone, my tears spent*, she thought. *Will I remain desolate and forsaken, with no hope?*

The cry of Rome was a thunderous roar in Rachel's mind. She had heard it hundreds of times—but never had it lain so heavily on her heart as now. *They're extinguishing the only ray of light in this darkness by burning the people who love one another, and they're too blind to see it.* In the swirling blasts of smoke above the

Colosseum, she was certain she saw the outline of a cross.

She would never attend the bloody theater again. It had sent her parents and her brother to their deaths, and it had sent her to her death in spirit.

That night, Rachel didn't sleep. Instead she read from her mother's copies of the Scriptures, internalizing the words hungrily. As she read, something mysterious happened. Rays of hope began seeping into her soul. She felt as though she were drinking from an everlasting, pure fountain. Before the night was over, Rachel came to belief.

Then something even more mysterious happened. As she submitted her will to God's, His Holy Spirit enabled her to do the impossible. She began to feel love in her heart for her grandfather.

On her balcony at dawn, Rachel lifted her hands to the sky. "Oh, Lord, thank you!" she murmured softly. "Now I know what I felt in the depths of my heart yesterday morning. You were gently pushing me to the Colosseum so I could understand your victory over the enemy of my soul. It brought me the rest of the way to you. You are more powerful than death.

"And finally I can understand what it is to forgive—to pardon someone for wrongs they've done. I know my grandfather has been cruel to us, but he is so warped with pride that he has no capacity left for love. Help me to show him."

CHAPTER TEN

I do wish I'd have more of the holy writings, Diana," Rachel said, lowering herself to the hearth beside her closest friend. "Then we could study all of it together. There is so much I don't understand."

Diana glanced up from the rough parchments with a smile. "These pages are all marked up, Rachel. Your mother must have pored over them."

"I noticed that too." Rachel leaned forward. "Look at these psalms that talk about fearing no evil in the shadow of death. She underlined a lot there."

Diana studied the words for a moment. "The words must have been precious to her."

"I like reading through the psalms best," Rachel admitted. "The poetic phrases capture my attention. 'To him that rideth upon the heavens of heavens, which were of old . . .' It isn't hard to memorize these powerful words. They strike a responding chord in the depths of my being."

Diana gave her a quick glance. "Rachel, you astound me. You're drinking all of this in like . . . like—"

"Like a hart panting after the water brooks?" finished Rachel with a laugh. "This is what I've been searching for all my life, Diana."

"So this faith answers your questions about the meaning of life?" Diana asked.

"Yes," Rachel said simply. "Jesus gives meaning to all of life."

Diana's expression was troubled. "You still don't know what your grandfather is going to say when he finds out you're a Christian. Doesn't that matter to you at all?"

Rachel's eyes clouded. "Of course it matters."

"Your grandfather is capable of doing anything to you," Diana stated, her words trembling slightly. "I'm worried about you, Rachel. So worried that I would plead with you to give up this faith if I only knew there's a chance you would."

Rachel drew back. "I didn't accept my faith just to give it up now."

"And that's what scares me." Diana stood up, pacing toward the window. "I have always admired you, Rachel. When you make up your mind about something, you always stand firm on it. But do you actually realize what it might cost you this time?"

"Diana, listen to me." Rachel looked into Diana's eyes. "I weighed the cost before I ever chose the Way. Death is only a door where I can meet God face to face and live with Him in glory forever. What my grandfather will do or say doesn't matter to me. I have given my life to God, and I am in His hands."

Diana gazed into Rachel's shining eyes for a long

moment. "All right, then," she said at last. "You've made up your mind, and I won't try to change it."

———————

What my grandfather will do or say doesn't matter to me. The words taunted Rachel as she moved slowly down the stairs. There was no denying the dread that weighed heavily on her heart now as she approached the triclinium. With all her being, she wanted to flee from what lay ahead.

Her grandfather was striding toward her, speaking over his shoulder. "The carriage is waiting, Cornelia. Just go on out. I will see if . . ." He had just seen Rachel. "There you are. I was about to call you. I want to arrive in the city as early as possible this morning for the celebration of Jupiter."

Rachel took a deep breath and straightened. "Father," she said quietly. "I don't want to go today."

Her grandfather stopped, his eyes widening. "You don't want to go?"

Rachel's eyes fell from his, the color deepening in her cheeks. "It's impossible for me to go with you, Father. I'm a Christian now, and I can't take part in the celebrations any longer."

"You, too?" The aged weariness in her grandfather's tone brought Rachel's head up. He wasn't even incensed?

"I've become convinced of the truth of the Christian faith," she said softly. "And now it is my faith as well."

Her grandfather was shaking his head slowly. "You don't know what you are saying, Rachel."

A strangled cry sounded behind him, causing Rachel's heart to jump. Cornelia stood there, her face ashen, her eyes filled with pain. "Oh, Rachel! How much can a mother bear?" She swayed weakly, and her husband reached out to steady her.

"Leave us at once, Rachel!" he ordered sharply. "Go to your chamber and stay there until you change your mind."

Tears blinded Rachel's vision as she stumbled up the stairs. "I could have taken everything else," she whispered. "But to hurt my grandmother like this . . . I can't stand it!"

In her room, she curled up on her bed and wept.

That afternoon, a sound came from the door leading to the balcony. *Tap-tap-tap*. "Rachel? May I come in?"

Rachel paled and stood up. "Justin?" He must have climbed the balcony steps to meet with her privately, rather than entering through the house.

"Am I disturbing you?" Justin asked.

"Not at all," Rachel said hesitantly, trying to decide if she could trust the man in front of her.

Justin came in and sank down on the stool next to the hearth. He closed his eyes. "When I saw you in the catacombs, I thought I must have been dreaming."

"It's a long story, Justin," Rachel said. "But I have accepted their faith as my own."

He shot her a penetrating glance. "I have time to listen to your story if you want to tell it."

Rachel hesitated. She didn't want to endanger her newfound family living in the catacombs.

"Rachel," Justin said quietly, "I don't condemn you for doing this—and I won't turn you in, I promise. You're my own cousin." His eyes met hers. "But you aren't safe here any longer. You must flee. And if you are caught after that—" He hesitated. "There is nothing I can do to help you."

"I know, Justin," answered Rachel, taking a deep breath. "But God lives in my heart, and His love for me takes my fear of death away. Justin, won't you let me tell you about the one living God?"

Justin held up a hand. "Rachel, please. Don't try to convert me. There's no way I could change now, even if I'd want to." He paused, and his voice was a mere whisper when he spoke again. "Which I don't."

Silence fell between them. Rachel watched her cousin's strong features shadowed with pain, evidence of the intense struggle within. "Tell me, Justin," she said at last. "How did you discover where the Christians were gathered in the catacombs?"

A muscle in Justin's jaw tightened. "Fabian was in contact with a fossor—enough to brainwash him and dig out of him everything he knew about the Christians. The fossor has since been eaten with remorse, but the damage is done. We captured thirty people because of what he told us."

Rachel shook her head slowly. "Fabian must be extremely hard-hearted. He's so determined to hunt down the Christians."

"You have to be hard-hearted for this work," Justin replied bluntly. "We're drilled that these people must be driven from our lands, and that there is no power on earth greater than Rome."

"Do you truly believe that?"

Justin didn't answer immediately. "How I think and feel is irrelevant," he said at length. "It's a work I must do, and that's that."

He glanced at her. "But, Rachel, I believe there is finally a chink in your grandfather's armor. He told your grandmother that his whole family is slipping, slowly but surely, from what he has worked to teach them all these years."

Rachel caught her breath. "He actually said that?"

"He did." Justin rose to his feet. "After hearing that, I believe he does have love somewhere in his heart for his family—almost as if he's resigned to their decisions instead of only wanting to punish them."

"Maybe you're right." Rachel followed Justin to the door. "Thanks for coming, Justin. I will consider your warning."

"Goodbye, Rachel." Gripping her hand, Justin looked into her eyes. "I have done all I can for you."

Then he was gone, leaving Rachel standing in the doorway. With a sigh, she turned back to the fire. "At least I got through the whole interview without mentioning the arranged marriage to Fabian," she said to herself. "I do not want to marry that man. But I have a feeling that the marriage is going to be dropped, now that I'm a Christian. It'll be the last thing on my grandfather's mind."

I do wonder what Fabian thought of the idea, though. Now if he would be like Philip Lucius . . . As the thought flashed through her mind, Rachel felt her face grow warm. *Though I haven't known Philip long, I think he's a very good man,* she acknowledged silently. *Fabian might know where he stands in what he believes, but Philip stands for God—and that's where the difference lies. Philip is spiritually strong. It shows because he chooses to live a dangerous life aboveground at the pottery shop. I can't understand how he has the courage.*

For a long moment she stared into the fire, watching the flames dance merrily on the hearth. "I wish I had more courage, Lord," she whispered. "I do so hate hurting my grandmother like this. But how I hope my grandfather's heart will be softened through his family's decisions to live for you!"

Picking up her mother's holy Scriptures, she read in John's Gospel, "Let not your heart be troubled . . . I will not leave you comfortless: I will come to you . . . He that hath my commandments, and keepeth them, he it is that loveth me."

Lifting her head, Rachel gazed out the window. "Thank you for meeting me here in my hour of need, Lord," she murmured. "You promised not to leave me comfortless, but to be my source of strength and courage as I choose to believe in you. With you at my side, I don't need to be troubled. I will rest in that fact."

Pardon's Price

Chapter Eleven

December 2, 258

My newfound peace is slipping, trying to gain a foothold in the avalanche around me. But the Lord keeps reminding me that all things are possible with Him. I certainly hope He has a plan.

Grandmother came up to my chamber and told me that Grandfather was advised by the Emperor to have me banished—that is, to let me meet the same fate of all the other Christians. She said that if it were up to him, he wouldn't use such drastic measures; but with the Emperor pushing him, he feels he has no choice. His pride won't let him appear weak in the eyes of all these witnesses.

Grandmother urged me to flee, so for the last few hours I've been packing. Mario sent Philip a message from me, and Philip sent word back that he would meet me at the peristyle gates after dark. So in just a few minutes my whole world will be changing.

I know where I'll be going—into the catacombs to my family.

"Well, Rachel, you've been here for over a month now. How are you feeling about everything?" Adara spoke gently.

Rachel didn't answer immediately. Finally she said slowly, "How should I feel? I've had quite a time adjusting to my new life, that's for sure. I've met many Christians here, and my family has grown dear to me. But it seems as though we'll never be able to span the gulf that all those years of separation have put between us."

"Of course it's hard," Adara said understandingly. "Your family was nothing more than mere strangers when you first met them."

"I appreciate the privilege God has granted in allowing me to meet them, of course," said Rachel. "But my mind keeps going back to my grandparents. I feel that nothing is finished—so many pieces of the puzzle aren't in place yet. Perhaps they never will be, but I can't help thinking that somehow . . ." She paused, collecting her thoughts. "Put it this way. I feel that I left too quickly."

Adara shook her head. "You had to flee, Rachel, to escape certain death."

"But am I not in God's hands?" Rachel's eyes flashed as she stepped toward Adara. "Shouldn't I simply have trusted Him to work everything out?"

"Rachel." Adara's voice was soft. "You're a Christian, and you have placed your life on the altar, have you not?

You *are* trusting God to work everything out. That doesn't mean you have to put yourself in the way of sure death."

Rachel took a deep breath. "I know you're right, Adara. But it's so hard to sit back and do nothing about my relationship with my grandparents."

"If God has something for you to do, He'll show you in His own perfect time." Adara stood up. "I have something I want to show you in my copies of the Scriptures. In Paul's letter to the Ephesians, he writes, 'Now unto him that is able to do exceeding abundantly above all that we ask or think, according to the power that worketh in us, unto him be glory in the church by Christ Jesus throughout all ages, world without end. Amen.' Isn't that beautiful?"

"Exceeding abundantly?" Rachel whispered.

"God doesn't lie," Adara answered simply.

"I can hardly grasp it," Rachel breathed. "Oh, Adara, these Scriptures must be full of promises the whole way through! I would love to read them all."

"You may read through Ephesians," Adara said. "I will gladly give you everything I have."

Rachel reached for the parchments, turning them over in her hands. "I have read through my mother's copies of the Scriptures so often, I know them all by heart. I can bring them to you if you want to read them."

"I would appreciate that," Adara said with a smile. "I never tire of reading the Scriptures. These catacombs have become like holy shrines because of such free access to the Word through so many Christians."

Rachel's eyes lit up. "Our meetings are inspiring to me. I love the singing, and I love to hear the preaching of the Word. I'm thankful God has revealed His love for me in this way. It's like a soothing balm on my heart."

Adara laughed softly. "It's that way for all of us. If it wouldn't be for our meetings, I'm not sure how any of us could keep going."

Before Rachel could answer, a small whirlwind of a girl hurtled through the entrance of the chamber. "Aquilina!" exclaimed Rachel, catching the little girl's arm. "What have you been doing?"

"I tried to slow her down," came a laughing voice near the entrance. Rachel glanced back as Adara exclaimed, "Philip! It's about time you showed up again. Your daughter wanted to see you again."

"And I wanted to see her," answered Philip with a grin. "I closed my shop early tonight so I could come here and stay with my little girl for the weekend." He glanced at Rachel and bowed slightly. "Rachel. Good to see you again."

"Hello, Philip." Rachel's heart began to pound. "I can't wait a minute longer to ask, sudden as it may seem. Please tell me—how are my grandparents doing?"

Philip's eyes sobered. "I can understand your urgency. And I'm afraid the news isn't very good."

"Tell me quickly," Rachel urged softly.

"Your grandmother," Philip explained. "She has been mourning for you, and her heart has been getting weaker. She is distant from her husband—she can't find it in her heart to forgive him, because she feels he's destroyed their whole family. She told me this herself."

Rachel looked at Adara. "There. You see why I feel the way I do?"

"But Rachel, I don't know that it's a good idea to try visiting your grandmother," Adara protested.

Philip looked at Rachel. "Have you been thinking about it?"

"I told Adara that I feel as though I can't just sit here and do nothing," answered Rachel quickly. "Your message confirms it."

Philip shook his head slowly. "It's too dangerous for you to go up there."

"But I must! My grandmother—"

"You need to make sure you hear God telling you to go," Adara said quietly. "You don't want to do it without His blessing on your journey."

"Adara's right, Rachel," Philip said. "Until God clearly shows you what to do, you should wait."

"How can you be so sure?" Rachel challenged.

"Rest in the Lord, and wait patiently for Him," quoted Philip evenly.

Rachel lowered her head. "Patience never was one of my virtues," she said at length. "I will try to wait."

Philip and Adara smiled at her. "God will show you at the right time, Rachel," Adara assured.

That night before she fell asleep, Rachel brooded, her thoughts twisting and turning. *I'm restless*, she admitted to herself. She longed for a ramble through the forest, a day spent at the market with her friends, and a myriad of other things that she missed in the world aboveground. She thought of how many of the Christians had a pallid color to their skin. She had no doubt that if she'd stay down here much longer, she would grow pallid as well. She wrinkled her nose at the thought. *I want to go up at least once with the men who visit the city at night and bring back supplies for us. But I know it's dangerous.*

Finally Rachel slipped to her knees beside the narrow cot and prayed until she felt a measure of peace.

"Who is a God like unto thee, that pardoneth iniquity, and passeth by the transgression of the remnant of his heritage? . . . He will turn again, he will have compassion upon us." The leader read the beautiful words of the prophet Micah as he opened the service for Rachel's baptismal day.

"God is a God of love, grace, and pardon, who cleanses mankind from sin and sets them free," he went on, his voice resounding in the vaulted chamber as he glanced at those about to be baptized. "It cost God His Son to give us this precious gift of salvation. You are sealing your vows to the Lord this day to serve in His kingdom forever."

It cost God His Son. Philip's message about her grandmother still lay heavily on Rachel's mind. The leader's words struck deeply, burning into her heart. Jesus' sacrifice had been painful—should she not be willing to encounter danger and pain to be a witness to her grandmother? Maybe this was God's answer to her question of leaving the catacombs.

Chapter Twelve

A re you sure about this, Rachel?" Flickering shadows danced across Philip's face, highlighting his furrowed brow as he held the flaming torch aloft. Standing up, Rachel faced him.

"I was awake a long time last night, reading the Scriptures and praying," she said quietly. "And I feel my answer is clear—God is telling me to go to my grandmother. It's something I feel deep inside that I can't explain, something that says I need to go *now*. My grandmother does not have a strong heart. What if all this turmoil takes her life before I have a chance to explain to her what has happened to me?"

"I don't like to see you put yourself in danger," answered Philip with concern.

"I'm not afraid," Rachel said steadily. "I'm placing my life in God's hands. I want to talk with Athena too, if it's possible to meet with her in secret. Will you help me,

Philip?"

"I can do that." He hesitated. "I just want you to be certain that you want to do this."

"I'm sure." Rachel met his gaze squarely. "I'm traveling with some of the men and boys here, so I'll get into the city safely. The rest is up to you."

"You can trust me," answered Philip, and he vanished into the darkness.

Silence descended on the small chamber. Katerina released a long breath and gave Rachel's shoulder a squeeze. "You do realize we may never see you again, don't you?" The trembling words were more a statement than a question.

Rachel placed her own hand over the slender one on her arm. "I will never forget these weeks, Katerina. The time I spent with all of you as my family will always be a treasured memory in my heart."

———◆———

The sun was setting in vivid shades of rose and burnt orange when the small group reached the city. The first sight of the sunset took Rachel's breath away. "Oh, I've missed this," she breathed, almost reverently. All the pent-up longing from those weeks in the catacombs spilled out and invested itself in the sights about her—the streets teeming with life at this evening hour, a din so great one nearly had to shout to be heard.

"You've missed the noisy crowds?" David asked from where he was walking beside her. The others had scattered, so as to make their group not so obvious in public. Rachel now walked only with Adara's son.

A faint smile played around Rachel's lips as she glanced at the tall youth. "Strange as it may seem, I have. I had a lot of good times wandering through this city with my friends—and my grandmother. It's good to see it all again."

A voice hailed them from the sidewalk. "I've been looking for you," Philip said, hurrying toward them. "The hour is getting late, and I was almost ready to close my shop. Why don't you all step inside?"

"Adara sends you greetings," Rachel said, stepping through the doorway. "And Aquilina sends you this."

"A package?" A twinkling sparkle flashed in Philip's eyes as he took it from her. "I'll look at this later. Rachel, Athena is in the back room of my shop. She agreed to meet you there. As for your grandmother—she will be coming with Diana later." Philip opened a door at the back of his shop. "When your grandmother heard you were coming, she was determined to meet with you, no matter what."

Rachel laughed softly. "I hoped she would. This will be better than trying to go home to talk with her."

As she walked into the back room, Rachel's gaze fell on a tall figure standing at the window, half-hidden by long curtains that draped to the floor. Athena stood there silently, the silky folds of her yellow tunic shimmering in the last rays of the sun. She turned slowly, her black eyes, formerly flashing with life, now dull and void of sparkle. They lit up when they fell on Rachel, however, and Rachel ran to her side. "Athena!"

"It really is you," Athena breathed. "Oh, Rachel, I was beginning to think—" She broke off as the tears came, and Rachel flung both arms around the slim shoulders.

"I'm here," she whispered in her ear.

Athena took a deep breath. "I never thought I'd see you

again, Rachel. You just disappeared and no one knew where you had gone. Bernice and I went to visit your grandmother, but we couldn't get anything out of her. I couldn't help but wonder—" She paused. "There were many speculations about why you left. Many wondered if you'd become a Christian."

"It's a long story, Athena, and we don't have much time to talk." The girls seated themselves on small stools, and Rachel went on. "Briefly—I left because I did indeed become a Christian, and my grandfather was going to have me banished. He was influenced by the Emperor and felt he had no choice. So I fled down into the catacombs, where I've been ever since."

Athena studied her intently. "So you did become a Christian. Does that account for the glow on your face?"

"I have a glow? I never heard that before. But if I do, it's because my life now has purpose," Rachel added softly. "Jesus Christ is my Lord and Savior. My whole life is in His hands, and I have joy in my heart like I've never known before. But now about you, Athena—how have you been doing?"

"Not so good." Athena sighed and looked at the floor. "I can't stop thinking about what happened to Cadmus. My whole future was in him, and now—" She sighed, her eyes drifting shut. "It's like there's nothing left—nothing worth living for. Many times I have wished I could die. Maybe I could join him then."

"Athena!" Rachel caught her arm. "Just because Cadmus died doesn't say that you have no future. You do. And you would see it too, if you only knew where to look."

"All right, Rachel." Athena's shoulders sagged. "So tell me. What do you have to say?"

Rachel took her hand. "Have you ever thought about trying the way of the cross? That is where the Christian's faith starts. We believe that Jesus died on a cross as a sacrifice for our sins, and then we follow Him wherever He leads us. This life is hard and never will be easy. But because we have God to help us, we can have peace. He promised to be everything to us—our help, shield, and defender. He is preparing an eternal home for us after death. Oh, Athena, I could talk all night about my God! All we have to do is believe in Him to be saved."

Athena shook her head slowly. "I don't know, Rachel. It sounds wonderful, but . . . I've been taught against it all my life, you know. To me the Christians have always been like a—a—curse."

"I know, Athena. Remember, I grew up with that too."

Athena straightened. "How *did* you become a Christian, Rachel?"

Rachel told her of how she had talked with her real mother before she died. She told of her mother's sacred parchments and the words of life and instruction in them. She told Athena of her struggle to accept the way of the cross, and of how she had finally come to belief.

"I see it more clearly now," Athena said in the darkening room. "And I'm sure your mother was a wonderful woman with strong beliefs. But I just don't know, Rachel . . . it's something I will have to think about."

Struck by a sudden thought, Rachel glanced down at the parchments she held in her hand. Her breath caught in her throat. Could she really do it? After all, this was her mother's gift to her, and it was sacred. She valued it as the ultimate treasure among her possessions.

But she had owned the holy writings for nearly two

months, and the most important worth they contained was stowed away in her heart. Before she could lose her courage, she held them out to Athena. "Won't you take these, Athena, and read them for yourself?"

Athena's eyes widened as she looked from the parchments to Rachel. "But this is from your mother. I can't take something that's so precious to you."

"I want you to, Athena," Rachel said steadily. "In the catacombs, many people have portions of the Scriptures, and I can borrow them. I won't force you to take it, but you're certainly free to."

Athena hesitated before taking the rough book and turning it over gently in her hands. "I'll take good care of it, Rachel, I promise. And someday, perhaps I can give it back to you again."

They left the room together, entering the shop where Philip was working at his desk. He glanced up as they approached. "Did you ladies have a good visit?"

Athena returned his smile. "Indeed we did. Thanks so much for letting us use your shop tonight. I'll see you later, Rachel."

"I can't figure out what is taking your grandmother and Diana so long to get here, Rachel," Philip said as the door closed behind Athena. "I thought they would have been here before now."

"I was wondering about it too." Rachel's forehead creased as she moved toward the window and glanced out into the street. It was lit up with lamps that glanced light off the stone pavement. "Could something have happened to prevent them from coming?"

"It's possible." Philip joined her at the window. "I'm not sure how safe it is for you to be standing right here,

Rachel. Suppose the wrong person sees you?"

"Suppose the wrong person sees *you*, Philip?" Rachel countered. "Sooner or later, you're going to be found out if you stay here."

He shrugged slightly and stepped back. "I'm not worried about that."

"But your daughter—"

"—Is in good hands," he finished. "And even more importantly, she's in God's hands. Rachel, even if the authorities discover who I am, I will not hide. I am in God's hands too. Now you must leave. The people you came with are probably waiting for you by now."

Rachel stepped toward the door. "Thank you for letting me use your shop tonight, Philip."

"God go with you," he answered, closing the door behind her.

How does he do it? Rachel shivered from the keen air as she stepped into the street and pulled her *palla* more tightly about her shoulders. *He must have God's protection around him. He's certainly brave—braver than I could ever be.*

A movement to the left caught Rachel's eye. Men were riding down the street on horses, their crimson uniforms glittering in the flickering lamplight, their swords glinting like steel. She gasped and whirled around just as a stern command came from behind her. "Interrogate this person."

"Yes, sir." The leading soldier reined in his horse next to the sidewalk and peered down at her. "It was reported to us that a group of Christians is here in this city tonight. Do you have any ideas—" He stopped abruptly. "Rachel?"

"Yes, Fabian." Rachel's gaze did not falter as she met his eyes.

Fabian studied her intently for a long moment. "So you appear again. But why are you here at this hour of the night? Your grandfather told me that you have blackened the family name."

Out of the corner of her eye, Rachel caught a glimpse of Justin among the soldiers, his face ashen. For a brief moment their eyes locked, and then Justin turned away, spurring his horse in the direction from where he had come. Rachel's throat tightened.

Fabian stared after him before turning back to her, his question low. "Are you a Christian, Rachel?"

"Yes, I am," answered Rachel calmly. And with the confession came a strength she had no idea she was even capable of possessing, a strength that buoyed up her courage and lifted her spirits. No matter what happened, she was ready.

Fabian studied her a moment longer and then exhaled a long breath, his words quiet. "You know, things would have been a lot better for you if you had just denied it."

"How can I deny the truth?" she countered.

He stood there silently, the muscles in his features tense, his dark eyes holding something that Rachel could not quite define. "You don't realize what you are getting into," he said finally.

"I'm not afraid." She paused before adding, "Many others have suffered before me. I cannot ask for anything less."

He nodded once and turned. "Place this girl under arrest."

Justin lashed his horse into a full gallop, his thoughts whirling as they bolted down the street. How could Rachel do this? He had warned her that if she was caught, he could do nothing to help her. Why had she so blatantly disregarded him?

His face contorted with anguish as he groaned aloud. As of tonight he was done capturing Christians. It was a work he simply wasn't cut out for, a distasteful business that he couldn't stomach. Perhaps, if he had the chance, he would even talk with Rachel—discover what it was about her faith that made it worth more than her life.

His eyes fell on two figures, dark silhouettes against the evening sky. They were inching down the street ahead of him, the taller one holding the other's arm. As Justin reached them, he reined in his horse sharply. "Aunt Cornelia!"

His aunt's face was framed by the hood she wore about her head, adding a somber darkness to the eyes that widened with apprehension as they met his. "Justin!" she exclaimed. "What are you doing here at this hour?"

"I was thinking I should ask *you* that." But as he noted that she was walking with Diana, he had no doubts about what they were doing here.

"You won't find Rachel, Aunt Cornelia," he said flatly. There was no point in prolonging the truth. "She was captured."

His aunt's face blanched, and Diana caught her arm, turning quickly to face Justin. "How do you know this, sir?"

Though her tone was respectful, Justin caught the warning in her eyes.

He nodded slightly in acknowledgment, his tone softening. "I'm sorry to put it so bluntly. But . . ." His voice trailed off and he turned away, suddenly unable to finish.

Stepping forward, Aunt Cornelia caught his arm with a strength that surprised him. "You must do something about this, Justin," she cried out.

"I will do what I can." But his heart sank as he said the words. He knew he could do nothing.

Long after the door closed behind her, Rachel paced the tiny cell. Face to face with death, she paused under the narrow window and gazed into the deep blue sky. Somewhere beyond those skies was a home prepared for the children of God. Would she really be there by this time tomorrow?

The trial in the early hours of the morning had not lasted long. When the magistrates discovered that Rachel stood firm in her faith and commitment to the God she served, they sentenced her to death in the Colosseum's arena at the mercy of wild beasts. She was to appear there the next day, in the afternoon.

She had not seen Justin again. Rachel shivered and turned away, pacing the small room once more. This was not how she had wanted things to turn out. If only there had been a way of breaking through to Justin, of helping him see the light through the darkness he found himself in.

She stopped pacing as a new thought struck her. She had strongly believed that she was to go to her grandmother—but why? Surely this was not the best way of sharing her faith with the elderly woman.

And then there was Diana. If only she could have

spoken once more with her. Depending on what she was thinking by now, perhaps—

Rachel shook herself. She was doomed to die, locked in a prison cell until the appointed time. There was nothing she could do to change that. Unless she recanted, she could not control her circumstances now.

A rap on the door broke into her reverie, and Rachel started. The door began to open slowly, revealing cold, hard armor. A soldier. But what could he want? A guard had delivered her morning meal only a couple hours before. She stood tensely in the center of the room.

But it was Justin who entered the room. Rachel sighed with relief. "Why are you here?"

"Rachel—" Justin caught her hands and faced her earnestly. "I have come to ask you to give up your faith. You've seen what the Christians face. How can you even think of doing this? I spoke with the general about this, Rachel. I pleaded with him to pardon you, but I could get nowhere. The Emperor has no mercy on a Christian, not even . . ." His voice trailed off.

"Perfect love casts out fear," Rachel said quietly. "I love Jesus too much to deny Him. I'm not afraid of death; it will only open heaven's door."

He looked at her intently. "How can you be so sure?"

Rachel searched his eyes. "Are you willing to listen to what I have to say?"

He closed his own eyes, his features contorting with anguish. "I feel wretched, Rachel," he admitted. "I'd give anything to get out of the position I'm in. I want nothing to do with hunting the Christians now. I've seen things that would make your blood run cold." He glanced sideways at her. "But you're not surprised to hear me say that, are you?"

"Christianity isn't easy, Justin. I know that as well as anyone."

"So . . . what's the secret?" he asked hesitantly. "I want to know what this faith is, Rachel. In fact, I—" He paced to the window and looked out. "I think there's something in it that heralds freedom. And I have to confess that even though I tried to set you free, I really want to be free myself. I've wanted it for years, but now I think I know where to look for it. Will you tell me what you know?"

"One question first." The hint of a smile played around Rachel's lips as she held up her hand. "Did you come down here to ask me this under the pretense of pleading with me to give up my faith?"

He met her gaze. "It was either that or never see you again."

"I can understand that," she said thoughtfully. "Listen, Justin, what I have to say can push you in the right direction, but in the end you'll have to choose for yourself."

"And I don't promise to change my beliefs," he answered seriously. "But I do want to know."

She smiled softly. "That's the best place to start."

CHAPTER THIRTEEN

Rachel had often thought about the moment she would face death. Would she be afraid? Calm? Joyful? Which emotion would control her spirit?

As the soldiers led her down the street, she felt saddened by the irony of the crowd's mood. Smiling and jovial now, they would soon become a fierce mob with an inhuman thirst for blood. Still, Rachel felt a simple peace that pervaded her whole being and gave her the sense of doing something very right.

Though she looked for him, she couldn't find her grandfather anywhere. She did notice Diana, standing alone on the outskirts of the crowd. She looked ill. As their eyes met, Rachel smiled faintly. Diana's eyes widened as she lifted a trembling hand in response.

Rachel swallowed hard. She would be the only Christian appearing in the arena today. The men and boys she had traveled with from the catacombs had all escaped.

Now as she watched the multitudes around her, Rachel sent a silent prayer heavenward. *Oh, Lord, I ask for your strength today. I don't have other Christians to accompany me; I'm on my own. But I know you will be with me, dear God. Give me courage—this is my plea.*

Diana struggled through the corridor of the Colosseum, fighting against the press of the crowd. Tears pushed constantly against her eyelids, but she held them back by sheer force of will.

She had been tremendously relieved when Mario told her that Cornelia would not be attending today. In fact, she had considered staying home herself—but to do that with the knowledge of what was going on at the Colosseum would be torture. Doubtless, it would be torture to witness Rachel's death, but she simply couldn't stay home.

A hand grasped her arm, and Diana jerked around sharply. Athena stood behind her, her face pale. "May I sit with you today, Diana?" she asked quietly.

Diana did not hesitate. The mutual knowledge of the coming events broke the stiffness of their unequal statuses. "I don't want to sit alone." She led the way through an arched column. "Shall we sit close to the corridor?"

Athena took a trembling breath. "As you wish."

They seated themselves in silence. Only once did Diana turn to query, "You didn't want to stay home today?"

Athena shuddered. "I couldn't."

Diana nodded silently.

They fell silent again, waiting without speaking. The

Colosseum reverberated with the thunder of shouting throngs and the roaring of wild beasts that came from the vivarium[7] below. Clowns, jugglers, and acrobats were dancing in the arena, introducing the shows for the day.

All this faded from Diana's senses as her mind traveled back to the night before. Justin had joined his uncle for the *cena*. After the meal, he had privately asked Diana to meet him at the horse stables, where he'd told her of Rachel's sentence. "She asked me to tell you that you have been more than a sister to her," he said. "She doesn't want you to be sad when you receive news of her death. She says she will pass on to eternal life, and she hopes you will believe in Jesus so that you will join her someday."

Now Diana wondered if Rachel realized the hopelessness of the request she had made. *Do not be sad.* How could that be possible?

The air in the arena was alive with expectancy. Diana felt the crowd's excitement as keenly as she felt the trembling throughout her whole body. Beside her, Athena gripped her seat until her knuckles were white, her face ashen as she stared unblinking toward the arena.

Diana's glance shifted momentarily toward the Senate, where she had picked out Julian Gallus among the men. He was calmly watching the arena, giving no hint that he knew what was about to happen. But Diana could not believe that he didn't know, or that he didn't care about it. It was his own granddaughter who would be appearing in mere seconds—surely the elderly man was not so hardhearted as not to care what was happening to her.

That is, if he had any heart at all. After Rachel's

---

[7] An enclosure where the ancient Romans kept wild animals used in their entertainments.

parents had died here, Diana couldn't help but wonder. Her gaze fell on the Praetorian soldiers as she turned away. Justin was there, obviously the most silent one of the group. What was he thinking? He had mentioned his visit with Rachel, and how she'd shared her faith with him—but there was no way of knowing what was going through his mind now.

A lion was stalking around the arena, its tail lashing as deep growls rumbled from his throat. It was one of the largest lions Diana had ever seen, with a full mane and powerful muscles rippling under a tawny coat. The lion paused and raised its head majestically, eyes raking across the crowd before sweeping toward the opposite side of the arena.

A tall, slender figure stepped into full view, moving slowly toward the center of the arena. Diana was taken aback when she realized that it was Rachel. They had dressed her in white, attempting to mock her by draping her in elegance before her execution. A collective gasp swept through the gallery as cries of admiration rose from the crowd.

Rachel hesitated momentarily and glanced upward. In the dark eyes that locked with hers, Diana recognized a silent message. *Farewell, dearest friend. Do not weep for me. I am going to glory!*

In fact, Rachel seemed to possess an unearthly tranquility that displayed itself in her bearing. Her eyes shifted past Diana, focusing on the sky above the Colosseum. In that moment she seemed to forget everything—the multitudes and her impending death, which was quickly approaching. The lion had seen her, and its growls were becoming louder as he advanced.

But Rachel did not notice the lion. Her eyes still on the sky above, she fell to her knees in the sand. Her features appeared transfigured with radiance, while triumphant tranquility filled the notes of the song that fell spontaneously from her lips. "Glory, honor, and praise to the King of Kings, who reigns—"

A deafening roar from the large lion drowned out the rest of the song as it sprang toward her with yellow eyes gleaming and both paws spread wide. A thick cloud of dust enveloped the unfolding scene below, hiding it from view for a moment. When it settled, the lion was standing over the mangled form of the fallen girl, blood dripping from its jaws.

Diana had seen enough. Rising unsteadily to her feet, she stumbled from the gallery. Only when she reached the empty corridor did she realize that the scream of terror surrounding her was coming from her own lips.

———————

Justin had never felt so helpless in his entire life. While he watched, his beloved cousin was being mangled. As he listened to the thunderous roar of approval from the multitude around him, a deadly anger crept into his heart. At that moment he could have slain every individual in the vast gallery without qualm, and without mercy. Even his uncle—no, especially his uncle. The man had surely known what was to happen. Didn't he care?

His jaw clenched as he rose to his feet. There was nothing more he wanted here.

The lion had stepped back from its prey, who lay still where she had fallen. Tears stung Justin's eyes as he turned and moved on. Rachel had shared her faith with him, and he had been intrigued—but now he wasn't so sure. Was the God she served harsh and cruel, with no mercy on those who believed in Him? He couldn't deny the peace and joy he had witnessed in the minutes prior to Rachel's death—it had radiated from her like a light shining in darkness. But was the way of the cross really worth it?

With a groan, he glanced upward. Twilight was falling. He remembered Rachel telling him once that twilight was one of her favorite times of the day. *She'll never watch it again.*

He stumbled into the forest, heading toward the river.

Gradually the purple shadows over the city deepened into dusk as stars began to appear. Rome lay in darkness.

PART TWO

CHAPTER FOURTEEN

W hat makes you sure you want to do this?" The words hovered between the pottery merchant and the young man in front of him, poignant with meaning. Philip did not lift his head as he spoke, his hands moving with skillful precision as he shaped a vessel from the clay on the table. His brother-in-law leaned against the edge nearby, trying to appear casual, but only succeeding in tensing the atmosphere of the room.

"It's my calling." Adelpho Lucan's tone was clipped, his dark eyes holding fire. He straightened abruptly, stepping toward the window. "I have a duty to serve my country." He turned back. "Can't you understand that?"

"It goes against the law of Christ."

"Leave your God out of this!" Adelpho's voice rose angrily. Finally he said passionately, "I know it could mean death, Philip. But it's a risk that every soldier must take."

"Adelpho," Philip tried again.

"Don't try to dissuade me, Philip." Adelpho's tone was sharp again, but he didn't care. He was tired of Philip's attitude. He had dreamed of being a soldier ever since childhood—even now he could see himself marching straight and proud down the city streets in the glittering scarlet uniform of the Roman soldier's attire, with mobs cheering and trumpets blaring. It was an enticing vision.

Except when Philip voiced his concern and threw cold water on his dreams.

Pushing back his chair, Philip rose slowly to his feet. The young man standing before him was muscular and well-built, with a handsome chisel to his features that did not escape Philip's artistic eye. But something in the flashing black eyes disturbed him. He had seen it often enough to realize what it meant, and he feared the consequences the young man's temper could bring upon himself.

But he also knew Adelpho well enough to realize that he was through discussing the matter. He clapped a friendly hand on the broad shoulder and spoke lightly. "Then I will ask God to go with you, brother."

Adelpho drew a deep breath, and the tension departed as a faint grin came to his lips. "You realize what saying those words here could mean, don't you?"

Philip smiled. "I'm not worried about that. Have a safe trip home."

It wasn't a light statement. The afternoon sun was already dipping toward the west, which meant Adelpho would be traveling well into the night.

Leaving the shop, Adelpho strode down the sidewalk, pausing for a moment to search the street. His sister Amata had promised to meet him here, but she was nowhere in sight. Of course, even if she would happen to be nearby, it was nearly impossible to see her in the throngs that crowded the streets. Every time he entered the city, he was amazed again at how busy it was.

The rhythmic beat of prancing hooves against cobblestone pavement caught Adelpho's attention. The figure seated atop the high wagon was a mere silhouette against the last rays of the setting sun, but the handsome team of black stallions earned audible praise from the bystanders as they cleared to let the wagon pass. Adelpho found himself straining for a better glimpse.

A lone horse and rider galloped up from the east, moving swiftly through the street. Adelpho could see by his uniform that he was a Roman soldier. "You there! Halt!" he shouted to the driver of the wagon. All eyes gazed at the unfolding scene.

Startled, the driver glanced back and then leaned forward quickly to lash his whip. But it was too late. The soldier, nearly upon the wagon, was already unsheathing his sword.

The young driver stood up in the wagon. As the soldier approached, he leaped to the ground, rolling clear of the thrashing hooves rising above him as one of the stallions reared, snorting and blowing through flared nostrils. Without a backward glance, the young man sprang to his feet and fled toward the forest.

Instant confusion broke out in the street as the soldier spurred his horse into a race after the fleeing figure and the team of stallions bolted with the wagon. Adelpho watched as several men took off after the runaway team, and he wondered if he should do the same. But no. If the soldier returned with the fugitive, he wanted to be there to see it. The young man was clearly running for his life—but why? Was he an escaped prisoner? Gladiator? Christian?

That thought was enough to halt him in his tracks. A Christian. A man like Philip, who was more upright than any other man he'd ever known, on the run? The soldier's intentions were clear: death to the young man if he failed to escape. How had the soldier discovered his identity, if indeed he was a Christian?

Concern for his own brother-in-law rooted itself deep in Adelpho's heart. If Philip was ever discovered, it would mean death. An innocent pottery merchant? Right—but so much more than that.

Slowly, he brought his gaze back to the street. Amata was standing on the outskirts of a small crowd of women and girls. As Adelpho approached, she turned and ran to him. "Did you see what happened?"

"Are the men back with the runaway team yet?" He parried her question with one of his own, searching the street intently.

At that moment the handsome team marched into view, controlled by shouting men. "I hope the young man escapes," Amata said quietly, her gaze returning to the forest.

"He might be a criminal, you know." Adelpho shot her a sideways glance. "They don't deserve—"

"That soldier intends to kill him, Adelpho," Amata broke in, her expression troubled. "No matter if he's a criminal or not, he's still a person."

Adelpho made no response to that. "We need to get going," he said instead, turning away. "We'll have a long night ahead of us if we wait any longer."

Amata fell into step beside him as he headed down the

sidewalk. The men had taken the team into a sparsely populated side street, leaving the horses tied at the hitching post as they disappeared within the *taberna*,[8] no doubt in search of an evening meal. Adelpho sauntered leisurely into the street, slowing as he approached the wagon. Though plain, it showed quality workmanship. The back of the wagon was freighted with sacks and crates, looming high in the dim light. The driver appeared to have processed an order for delivery.

"Adelpho?" Amata's voice at his shoulder was soft. "Come and have a look at this."

Adelpho turned back. His sister was gesturing toward the dark depths of the interior under the driver's seat, her blue eyes holding alarm. "There's something there."

"Under there?" Adelpho stepped closer and bent slightly, searching the dark recesses of the space under the seat. His eyes widened. "Why is this here?"

"And not with the other crates and sacks? I have no idea." Amata straightened and gave him a knowing glance. "Do you think that young man was a Christian? I've heard—"

Adelpho placed one finger on his lips and gave his head a quick, almost imperceptible shake. Amata paled and fell silent, instantly comprehending his message.

"I don't think they saw this," Adelpho said slowly. Reaching out, he grasped the sack and pulled it farther into the light. It was narrow, long, and heavy. He glanced at Amata. "There's no way of knowing for sure, but—"

Amata glanced around. "Should we look into it?"

Adelpho hesitated. "I think we should find out what it

---

[8] A single-room shop within a large indoor market.

is," he said finally. "Let's take it with us in our wagon and inspect it after we're out of the city. I'll go get the wagon if you stay here."

Amata nodded. "I'll keep watch."

He smiled at her briefly. "I'll be back soon." With that, he was gone.

———————

The moon hung low in the night sky, cresting the sea waves with sparkling silver. Adelpho lashed the horses into a gallop as he entered the shore road, his mind whirling. Beside him, Amata turned slightly and glanced back into the dark recesses of the wagon. "I wish we knew more about what we're getting into."

Adelpho didn't answer. It had taken only a few minutes to bring his team to the sidewalk where Amata waited beside the runaway horses and the wagon with its precious cargo near the *taberna*. After they transferred the sack to their wagon, they had opened it furtively, just enough to confirm their suspicions. It was a body, wrapped in blood-stained cloth from head to foot. It lay silent and unmoving, convincing Adelpho that all life had departed. The sack was wedged into the full-length back seat of the wagon. Just before they had set off, Amata glanced back and gasped. "Wait, I . . . I saw something move."

Adelpho shot her a startled glance. "What do you mean?"

She was studying the sack intently. "It was so faint, I almost didn't think . . . and yet—it was a slight rising and falling movement, as if there was a slight breath. Could this person still be alive? I could be wrong, but—"

Adelpho's brow furrowed. "It wouldn't hurt to check, but we can't do it here. Once we're on the shore road, perhaps. Right now we've got to get out of this place. Those men will be back any minute."

And, indeed, the men were coming around the corner just as Adelpho seated himself on the wagon and flicked the reins. As they moved down the street, Amata twisted to look back. "No one's paying attention to us."

"Good. We'll stop as soon as we're able and check this out."

The search revealed a young woman. Dry blood crusted the black hair that framed her ashen face. They found a pulse on her neck—faint and irregular, but still beating. "We've got to get her to a physician as fast as we can!" Adelpho exclaimed.

"I think this young woman must have been a Christian who was thrown to the beasts in the arena," Amata declared. "Why else would that man have been taking off with her? I've heard that Christians take the bodies of their dead and bury them in the catacombs. It's possible the young man had those intentions." She glanced back, noting the young woman's facial features. "Adelpho, she's beautiful!"

Adelpho's hands tightened on the reins. "You didn't see more than just her face."

"What do you mean?"

"Her legs were mangled, Amata—a bloody mass of flesh. I don't know if she'll ever be able to walk again."

PARDON'S PRICE

Chapter Fifteen

The villa was more silent and still than Diana had ever known it to be.

She paused halfway down the stairs, the sound of her own footsteps dying away as she listened intently. Normally, at this early hour the place bustled with slaves scurrying about, performing their morning duties. But now the atmosphere seemed to be holding its breath, as though afraid of breaking a spell.

A door closed somewhere behind her, and Diana turned to see Jovan walking down the hall. "The mistress isn't feeling well this morning, Diana," he said softly, pausing beside her.

"Again?" Diana closed her eyes for a moment, massaging her temples with the tips of her fingers. "I thought she was doing better."

Jovan's dark eyes were somber. "The master is worried."

Diana could feel herself tensing. "Where is she now,

Jovan?"

"In her room. She was asking for you."

Diana moved on down the stairs, her steps dragging as she approached the floor below. No doubt she should check on the mistress, but she hated to do it. Who knew what she would find?

The senator was just closing the door behind him when Diana reached the chamber. He and the physician were talking in low tones. "It's not looking good, doctor. My wife has severe chest pain."

Diana stopped. Neither of the men had seen her, and she fought the impulse to flee. She had no desire to see the senator—the man who had done nothing to defend his granddaughter.

She pushed the painful thought away with effort and moved forward. "Excuse me, sir."

The senator turned, noticing her for the first time. "Stop right there, Diana. You can't go into that room."

"She sent for me, sir," Diana answered quietly, and waited.

"She isn't fit for visitors, ma'am." The physician spoke in a tone that bided no argument, and Diana said nothing more.

Drawing a quick breath of relief, she escaped down the hall and headed toward the kitchen. A slave girl named Ruth was there alone, kneading bread dough at a small table. "About time you showed up," she remarked as Diana appeared in the doorway. "Where were you?"

"The mistress sent for me." Diana came into the room and seized the poker next to the hearth. "But when I went down there, the physician wouldn't allow me to go into her room." A shower of sparks danced up from the hearth as she stoked the fire. "The senator said she had chest pain during the night."

"She is worse now?" Ruth's hands stilled. Though she hadn't been a slave here long, she and Diana had already become close friends. Since Rachel had fled to the catacombs, Diana did more work in the kitchen, no longer being responsible for Rachel's care.

Diana hesitated before setting the poker aside. "I don't think—"

Ruth gave her a quick glance as Diana paused. "What did the physician say?"

"She's not fit for visitors. That was all. But she had summoned me, and—" Diana shrugged. "I can't go to her now, I suppose."

"I wish you would," Ruth said softly. "She knows about Rachel's death."

Diana's eyes widened. "She does? But how?"

Ruth didn't answer immediately. Turning away, she stared out the window. "Justin told her about it last night."

There was no need for Ruth to say more. "I'll go to her as soon as I'm able to," Diana said quietly.

———————⧫———————

Diana shuddered as she listened to the pain-filled words.

"He doesn't even seem to care what is happening to our family. Sometimes I wonder . . ." The elderly woman's voice trailed off, and she shifted restlessly on the bed. "What would he do if everyone passed on and he was left alone?"

Diana made no response. She had wondered the same thing.

Cornelia Gallus was fading fast, there was no question of that. *It'll be a miracle if she lives through the night,* Diana mused as she took the slim hand.

"Rachel was ready to die," she said gently. "Never doubt that for a minute."

Cornelia searched her eyes. "Do you trust in her faith?"

Diana shook her head slowly. "She explained it to me, but—"

"I wanted to ask her about it," Cornelia said softly. "But I was afraid . . . of what it would do to me, to the life I've built with my husband. I could see the courage and purpose it gave to Rachel, and I greatly admired her, but I didn't feel ready. Tell me, what did she do in the arena?"

Diana swallowed hard and managed a smile. "She lifted her hands and sang a song about how the King of Kings reigns. That was all before the lion attacked. She was radiant with joy; you don't need to worry that her faith wasn't real."

"I know it was real." Cornelia took a deep breath. "Diana, please. Tell me everything you can remember Rachel telling you about her faith."

———◆———

For several hours, Cornelia remained still, her eyes closed, her lips moving intermittently. Diana stayed by her side until she took her last breath. A smile rested on her face then, as though she beheld a celestial vision.

Diana knew the elderly woman had passed on to meet her granddaughter.

Chapter Sixteen

Diana stood well back from the crowd standing in front of the sepulcher, folding her arms tightly to ward off the chill that persisted in spreading throughout her body. But she could not keep it from wrapping around her heart.

Her eyes lingered on the elderly man at the front of the crowd, standing stiffly silent with his head bowed. What was he thinking?

A hand touched her shoulder, and Diana turned to find Mario next to her. "You okay?" he asked in a low tone.

"I . . . will be." She glanced back toward Julian Gallus, and Mario's gaze followed. His grip on her arm tightened.

"He's going to be a lonely man," Mario said.

Diana's jaw set. "He asked for it."

Mario straightened, running long fingers through his black hair. "Whether he did or not isn't really important now. He'll need companionship in the coming weeks."

Diana shot him a glance. "Why do you say that?"

"He's disturbed," Mario answered. "He's still crying out in his sleep at night."

Diana shuddered and turned away, casting a quick glance upward. The day was overcast, with pearly gray skies that appeared as bleak as her own heart felt. When would this nightmare end?

Diana and Ruth worked side by side, preparing platters of steaming meals to distribute among the guests in the triclinium. Many had come to be with the senator on the evening of his wife's funeral, but Diana wouldn't necessarily have called it a sorrowful gathering. It was more like a festival.

Julian, however, remained silent, seemingly unaffected by the laughter and joviality swirling around him. Diana, covertly observing him as she placed a tray of fruit on the table, was frightened at the blank expression in his eyes. He appeared to be walking in his sleep.

As she turned away, Diana caught sight of Justin standing inside the room. The soldier's face was ashen, his eyes burning pools of pain—and something else. What was going through his mind?

At that moment, Justin's glance met hers. Diana shuddered and turned away. His hollow gaze emanated depression.

The look haunted her dreams that night, causing her body to toss in restless sleep. Once she awakened with a start, sitting straight up in bed. The night was as dark and still as the villa itself, with stars reflecting light against the window glass. There seemed nothing amiss, but Diana could not shake off a sense of foreboding.

A hoarse cry erupted through the wall, and Diana's scalp prickled. That was what had intruded into her slumber! Was it actually coming from the senator's chambers?

The door of her room glided open noiselessly, and Ruth appeared, a candle in one hand. "May I stay with you the rest of the night, Diana?" she whispered, crossing to the bed. "The master is frightening me; his sleep must be haunted."

Diana listened intently for a moment. "Is there anyone with him?"

"It seems like there ought to be." Ruth blew out the candle and placed it on the dressing table. "But he has done this before, hasn't he?"

Diana started to answer but halted abruptly. "Ruth—listen!"

The hoarse cry had risen to a scream, bouncing off the walls and shattering the silence of the villa. Ruth was at Diana's side in one bound. "What should we do?" she gasped.

Diana was already throwing back the bed covers. "I'm going for Mario," she tossed over her shoulder. "The senator needs help."

"What do you mean?" Ruth caught her arm, stopping her in the doorway.

"He needs help before he harms himself," answered Diana urgently, turning to face her. "Or someone else."

A minute after Diana left, Ruth heard shuffling footsteps in the hallway. Terrified, she made sure the door was barred. The footsteps faded until she could no longer hear them. Glancing out the window into the courtyard below, she saw a stooped figure slowly walking away from the house. She watched carefully. When Diana came back, she said urgently, "Diana! Tell Mario I saw the master leave the property. I can tell you the direction he went."

Justin stood on the banks of the river, gazing out across the waves that were coming to shore in a gentle tide. At this midnight hour, the moon was bright, creating a path of light across the water. Stars studded the sky far above, their reflections glancing off the waves in sparkling showers of jewels.

But the beauty of the night was lost to the young man standing on the shore.

The silent cry of his heart seemed to fill the vast expanse of sky and sea around him. Depression had plunged his spirits to the lowest depths of darkness and gloom. Life was a bitter existence, inhabited by demons of hatred and loneliness. The people around him lived only for violence and cruelty, caught in a vicious whirlpool that sucked them slowly into a pit. Would it not be best to simply end it all, especially since he felt he could no longer endure being a soldier? Life had utterly lost meaning.

Rachel had been like a sister. Yes, they had drifted apart as they grew older, but Justin supposed that was only natural—she was a young woman, after all, and he had become a man. Rome required much from its citizens, especially those in the army. He had occasionally been gone for weeks at a time, called to duty on the battlefield. He was well-respected among his peers, and he was the pride of his parents.

But life was empty—vain and void of purpose, dreary and bleak in its reality. In the midst of the gaiety that had swirled around him only hours before, he had understood that to the fullest extent. Everyone else was also searching, desperate to fill longings that could not be found through indulging in pleasure.

He had told no one, as yet, about his decision to withdraw from the work of hunting the Christians. He shuddered and shook his head, slamming the door on the rush of memories that followed. But it was not that simple. Images of Rachel flashed across the stage of his mind—Rachel, her eyes wide with fear and apprehension as she stood in the vaulted chamber of the catacombs . . . standing in the cold cell, explaining to him the way of the cross . . . graceful and strikingly beautiful as she moved toward the center of the arena . . . lying silent and still in death as the lion stepped back from its prey.

A great force of emotion welled up within him. He sat down on a rock and wept until his inner storm was spent. Then, quietly, he gazed out over the river as the tranquility of the waves fell like soothing balm on his bleeding soul.

A figure silhouetted against the outcropping of a rock some distance away caught Justin's attention. It was hunched slightly in a prostrate posture, the moonlight illuminating his face. As he studied the shadowy form, Justin felt the air leave his lungs. *Uncle Julian! What is he doing here?*

Slowly, he rose to his feet and then halted as a second dark figure emerged into the light. The movements of this figure were cautious and furtive, and as Justin studied the tall, powerful build of the man, he wondered if he should warn his uncle. But then the figure turned, allowing soft moonlight to illuminate his face for a moment—and in that split second, Justin recognized Mario.

A rush of awe swept through him. Somehow, in a way he could not even begin to fathom, his uncle's slaves cared enough about their master to follow him and protect him from the danger the man faced—a danger Justin could understand now as he watched. And with this understanding came a firm resolve.

If his life was to have any purpose at all, it would be in the realm of protecting people, not trying to end their lives.

CHAPTER SEVENTEEN

W hat are you going to do, Dr. Marcus?" Adelpho asked.

Their physician, a family friend, straightened slowly. He ran a weary hand through his hair. "If I would only know to what extent the danger is, I could better determine . . ." He paused. "I have fought for this girl's life for two days. Her pulse is stronger now, but those legs—something must be done."

Adelpho looked at his father, who was shaking his head. "It's a tough decision," Aelius Lucan said.

The physician nodded. "The wisest thing seems to be amputation, but I hate to do it. The operation is serious, and even if it were successful, she couldn't live a normal life."

"You must do something," pleaded Amata softly. "She thrashed and tossed all night in pain."

The physician's brow furrowed. "It might be better if she

would have died, rather than suffer this way. Do any of you know who she is?"

"They brought her here from Rome." Lydia Lucan spoke of her son and daughter. "Nobody knows if she was actually from there or not."

The physician nodded and straightened slowly. "I would kindly ask to be left alone in this room for a few minutes. I need to pray about this."

"We understand." Aelius took his wife's arm and turned, beckoning to Adelpho and Amata. Though he didn't share the physician's beliefs, Adelpho knew his father highly respected Marcus and his faith.

At the thought of faith, Adelpho's thoughts returned to his brother-in-law. Philip said that his God was filled with love and mercy toward His followers. But where was mercy in what had happened to this young woman? He certainly couldn't see it.

"Be careful with them, Alexander. And make sure they understand what is expected of them."

"Yes, sir." The tall man called Alexander turned and raised his voice to a shout. "Move along, you filthy slaves! Get on now!"

So this was the school where they trained criminals, slaves, and prisoners of war as gladiators. Mario's heart burned with anger as he marched into the gymnasium along with the other men. He had been taken without warning, sold from Julian Gallus's property and hurried away with no opportunity to say goodbye to Diana, his only known relative.

He could faintly remember the first time he was captured. It was fifteen years ago, when he was just five years old. The Romans had invaded his home city and taken captive those they did not kill. He recalled stumbling down the street behind the tall soldier, tears blinding his vision. He had never seen his parents again.

What a comfort it had been when he'd discovered Diana on the same ship he traveled on, bound for Rome. It was a miracle that they had never been separated all these years. They had grown to depend on each other. What would he have done without her?

"Where do you hail from?" The soft words sounded strange, coming as they were from such a giant of a man.

Mario turned to face him, noting the tall, muscular form and blond hair. "From here in Rome," he answered noncommittally.

The blue eyes regarded him quietly. "I am from the region of Gaul, just north of Italy. A barbarian—a prisoner of war. The Romans invaded my city and took many captive."

Mario caught the deep sadness in those blue eyes. "Romans are not merciful. I know how you feel. I was captured in Greece when I was a child."

The young man nodded. "No doubt you have seen much horror."

"You will see Rome at its worst if you live here long enough," Mario said dryly.

The giant did not flinch. "I am ready and willing to die representing Gaul, if that's what it takes."

Mario turned, studying him closely for the first time. "The trainers will be pleased with you," he said frankly. "I know enough about them to know they will not let you off easily. They will see your strength and train you as well as they can."

"And what do they want in return?" the other man asked slowly.

Mario shrugged slightly. "Wealth. Fame. You'll be at their mercy." He paused. "We all will."

The words hung between them, resounding in Mario's heart. Sudden resolve squared his shoulders and lifted his head. Let them do as they pleased with him. He wanted to live, to be free. If he must fight, he would fight for his freedom. There was no other way.

———◆———

When he entered the kitchen after chores, Adelpho found his mother standing at the hearth, stirring something in a kettle. "Sit down and let me get you something to warm your insides," she said, turning from the fire. "It's cold out there this morning."

"Thanks, Mother." Adelpho stood beside the fire, holding out his hands to its warmth. "My hands are so cold, they're numb."

"It goes with farming." Lydia ladled a bowl of porridge for her son. "This will warm you."

"How is our patient?" Adelpho asked, glancing toward the closed door off the kitchen. "Any better this morning?"

His mother's brow furrowed. "Did hear her during the night? For a few hours we gave her up for lost. But then her raging fever broke, and she pulled through."

"And Marcus thinks the operation was successful?"

"It's a little early to tell yet, but she is stable." His mother set a glass of wine before him. "Will your father be coming in soon?"

"He was feeding a newborn calf." Adelpho sipped his wine. "It was very sickly-looking. I'm not sure that it's going to live."

"Your father seems to be a natural when it comes to animals," Lydia remarked. "He usually makes them thrive."

"Well, that isn't me." Adelpho shifted restlessly. "Mother, sometimes I wish I could simply quit."

"Quit farming?" Lydia raised her eyebrows. "But Father has his heart set on you."

"I don't want to be a farmer all my life, Mother," Adelpho broke in. "And I don't want to stay on this farm all my life."

Lydia's expression was troubled. "You still want to be a soldier?"

Adelpho met her eyes. "Mother, I see no other choice. It's my calling, my duty as a man. I want to serve my country."

"But to maim and kill, my son—"

"I can take it. I'm not as weak as you might think." Adelpho shrugged. "It's part of the army, that's all."

"I wish you'd talk to Philip about this."

"I have." Adelpho sighed and leaned back in his chair. "He keeps talking about his God to me—how fighting goes against the law of Christ, and so on. But it's what every soldier has to face. And I intend to be brave, Mother."

Lydia shook her head. "I don't like it, Adelpho. I want you here with us for a couple of years yet."

"Father doesn't object. He understands how I feel. Rome is declining, you know. We need men who are willing to give their lives for the cause of saving it. Joining the army is the least I can do for the country I love."

"You really believe that?"

"It's the least I can do," he repeated.

His mother drew a deep breath. "Then I won't stand in your way, my son. But I will watch and wait for you." She stirred and rose to her feet. "I need to check on the young woman."

"Has Marcus found out who she is?" Adelpho drained the last of his wine and rose as well.

His mother shook her head. "No, he doesn't, but he's certain she was mauled by a beast in the Colosseum. He'll be able to find out who she is eventually, but he has to be careful who he asks."

CHAPTER EIGHTEEN

Justin paused before the shop at the corner, scanning the notice of the next day's gladiator show posted on the wall. He shook his head, feeling increasingly disgusted at the festivities. At his side, Fabian eyed him with a frown. "Why the sudden interest in a poster about a gladiator show?"

Justin shrugged his shoulders. "Tell me honestly, Fabian, what enjoyment do you get out of those shows?"

Fabian shot him a keen glance. "A lot more than you do, apparently. What's gotten into you? You've been acting strange for a while. I'm beginning to wonder if you have a problem with fulfilling your duties as a soldier." He paused and his eyes darkened.

Justin evaded the question. "I've got to get going," he muttered, turning away. But Fabian caught his arm, twisting him around again.

"Listen to me, Justin. What you need is to forget for a

while—get out and have some fun, rather than sit at home and mope all night. Come to the gladiator feast tonight. Celebrate with those who are about to die!" he finished with a sardonic smile.

After a moment, Justin said quietly, "I don't want to go, Fabian."

Fabian's grip tightened. "Justin, you've got to focus on having a good time."

Justin jerked his hand free. "You don't understand, Fabian." Anger edged his words. "There is nothing about the Colosseum and the gladiators that intrigues me anymore. Absolutely nothing."

Fabian's gaze did not waver. "You think so. You're sad right now, and you believe that all the old interests are dead. But give it time."

"Never!" Justin tore the poster viciously from the wall and ripped it into tiny shreds, scattering them in the street.

Silently, Fabian stared from him to the torn poster. "Then go home," he said at last, without looking up. "Go home and shut yourself away. I won't bother you again."

Justin stared after Fabian as he strode away without another word. The anger in his heart slowly melted, becoming tears in his eyes. A soft March drizzle pelted the pavement as he stepped from the sidewalk and moved down the street. Wrapping his cloak around him, Justin hunched his shoulders against the wind and lowered his head, his steps as slow as an elderly man's.

That morning his mother had said to him, "You can't go on like this, my son. Rachel might have met her death, but that doesn't mean you should. You've got to accept it and move on with your life."

Move on with life? There was no life. No future. Only aching yesterdays that mocked him and haunted all his waking moments—not to mention his dreams. No doubt he was a coward. He should be braver—tougher. After all, Christians were killed all the time.

———◆———

Diana stood alone in the kitchen, tears dripping into the soapy water she was using to scrub the evening meal's pots and pans. The silence echoed through the hallways and spacious rooms of the villa, weighing her spirits low.

She could still remember that awful day as though it had been only yesterday, when Julian Gallus sold most of his slaves in a single hour to slave traders with wolf's eyes. She knew their greed, their lust for power, and their cruelty. Diana shuddered and lifted the last scoured pot from the water, placing it on the counter nearby.

Why the master had not sold her was still a mystery to Diana. She hadn't known that Julian was considering selling his slaves, and the hour had come like the sudden blast of a trumpet—without warning, and certainly with no chance of saying goodbye to those she loved most dearly. They'd all been snatched away in a moment, leaving only silence.

All this had taken place two months ago. As Diana dumped the water out the back door, she wondered if she would ever see Mario again. She had no idea where he'd gone, and there was likely no way of finding out.

Life has changed too fast. Straightening, she gazed toward the distant horizon, where the sun was setting in shades of vivid red and gold, mixed with hues of lavender.

First it was Rachel, and then Mario, Ruth, and Jovan. Why am I still here?

With a heavy sigh, Diana stepped back into the kitchen and then stopped short, surprised. Justin had appeared around the corner.

"I thought I'd find you here," he said.

"What is it, sir?" she asked, closing the door behind her.

He seemed to hesitate, choosing his words carefully. "I thought you should know that Mario . . ." He paused as her head jerked up. "He—he is . . ."

"Tell me," she said quietly, throwing all respectful terms to the wind.

"He's at the feast tonight held for the gladiators," Justin spoke in a rush. "He was trained as a gladiator for the games tomorrow. I thought you should know about it."

Diana felt the air leave her lungs. She stared at Justin, denying his message even as it sank into her comprehension. "Oh, no . . ."

"If you want to see him—"

"Yes, I do." She whirled around, raising her voice. "Martha!"

"Yes, Diana?" The elderly housekeeper came to the doorway.

"Please finish the work here for me!" Without waiting for a reply, Diana slammed the door shut behind her and was gone.

"How did you find out about this?" Diana asked Justin on their silent ride through the streets.

A muscle in his cheek tightened. "Fabian told me."

"Fabian?" Diana's head came up. She despised that man, especially after he'd arrested Rachel.

"He stopped me when I was passing by the building where the feast is being held," explained Justin. "I never intended to go to the feast, but I knew then that I had to tell you about it."

"Tell me, sir, how did Fabian feel about Rachel?"

Justin shrugged. "I can't see inside his heart. He locks it away."

It wasn't an answer at all. Diana focused on the street ahead, where people were flocking into the gymnasium. "Who really does show their hearts?" she asked softly.

Justin reined in the stallion. "A Roman never does. You can get off here if you wish, Diana."

Diana stepped down from the wagon and joined the flow of the throng. Pulsating music vibrated the pavement of the street, and she could sense the excitement that pervaded the atmosphere around her. She had never been at a feast like this before, where the gladiators, ready for the upcoming battle, were set up like livestock for auction. They were giants of men, with powerful, muscular builds. They were guarded closely, but that did not hide the smoldering anger in their eyes as they surveyed the crowds.

Diana pressed her way through, searching for the only face that mattered.

At last she found him—lounging on a sofa in a corner with a glass of wine in one hand, well back from the crowds. His guard appeared to be half asleep and paid no attention when Diana slipped close. "Mario?"

He started, his eyes widening as they fell upon her. "Diana!" he whispered harshly, sitting upright. "What are you doing here?"

"Justin told me you were here," she answered, fighting back tears that threatened to spill. "Oh, Mario, I hate Rome!"

Mario placed one finger on his lips, his glance flicking meaningfully toward the guard. Diana lowered her voice to a whisper that reached only his ears. "Is there no way you can escape?"

He shook his head. "It's impossible, Di," he answered softly. "But listen—I intend to fight. I must, to gain my freedom. And I will gain it."

"That's only hope talking," she countered, her voice breaking.

"I'll fight to my dying breath to be free," he rejoined fiercely. "That takes more than just hope." He pressed her hand gently and whispered, "You better leave now."

She swallowed hard. "I'll be there tomorrow. Goodbye, Mario." The words caught and she turned, hurrying away before the tears spilled out. She didn't want *that* to be Mario's last memory of her.

Slowing, Diana turned back for one last look. Mario was still watching her. With a smile, he lifted his glass to her and saluted as if in victory.

But would it be?

That question burned in her heart all evening.

———◆———

"Romans! Imperial Rome! I bring to you the combat of the gladiators!"

The announcement was temporarily drowned out in the clapping and cheers that greeted the words. As it died away, the attendant thundered, "Men who will fight to the death—to the glory and strength of Rome!"

The cheers and clapping swelled in a great tide as trumpets heralded the gladiators marching toward the center of the arena. Halting beneath the Emperor's box, they raised their right arms in greeting. "Hail, Emperor! We who are about to die salute thee!"

Emperor Valerian looked down upon the gladiators, his lips curling into a grin. Leaning forward, he shouted, "You may proceed!"

Mario tore into his opponent with a red-eyed vengeance, venting his hatred against the roaring throngs, against the Emperor, against Rome itself. In the strength of his fury, the gladiator who met his sword fell, leaving Mario's hand and the hilt of the sword covered in blood.

The thunder of the multitudes resounded around the Colosseum as he stood over the fallen foe for a moment, victorious in the battle. Then he noted the twisted face, distorted in the agony of death. Suddenly he felt horror at what he had done. He flung the sword aside and fled from the arena, his steps faltering. A sob broke from his lips just as he reached the inside of the exiting corridor.

"My son." A hand touched his arm gently, and Mario's head jerked up as the soft voice went on. "You seem troubled. May I be of service?"

Mario's glance fell on the slight man standing at his side, his eyes filled with compassion as they gazed upon him. "I don't know how you could be," Mario answered darkly.

"I'm sentenced to die today in the arena," the man told him softly. "You are worried about the possibility of dying too—yes?"

Mario gave a short, bitter laugh. "Of course." His fist clenched. "I have been trained. Brutally forced to show my strength, brutally forced to fight this battle. I've vowed to win my freedom, or die trying."

"You are looking in the wrong place for freedom, my son." The man's voice was steady. "Jesus died on the cross to pay the penalty for your sins so that you can go free and gain eternal life."

"The cross?" Mario spit out the words. "The cross brings nothing but death!"

"To sin and self, yes. But it opens the door to salvation and eternal life. Jesus Himself said, 'And whosoever doth not bear his cross, and come after me, cannot be my disciple.' Will you not accept Jesus' forgiveness and gain eternal life in glory with Him while you still have the chance?" the man asked urgently. "You may not have another."

"I have just killed a man," Mario acknowledged heavily.

"God's grace and forgiveness are still free, my son. Believe in Jesus now while you have the chance. You can't afford to wait!"

The grille of the dungeon clanged open, and the attendant entered. "You there, slave," he barked. "Get up and come with me."

Mario glanced from the peaceful man to the attendant. "Yes, sir." Then he turned back to the other man, whose earnest gaze met his. Mario paused before he left with the attendant. "I appreciate your words, sir," he said softly. "Farewell."

"Farewell, my son. I will pray for you."

———◆———

As though hypnotized, Diana sat frozen in her seat as she watched the battle below. Gladiators fighting for the glory of Rome? No! A thousand times, no! Of all the sins in the world, what took place in the Colosseum had to be the most wicked and the least glorious. Where was mercy? Compassion? Did it even exist in this city that ruled the world?

The arena was cleared of dead bodies and blood, and a trumpet blast sounded. Mario entered the arena for the second time, striding straight toward the center with a firm, purposeful step. On the opposite side, another gladiator approached, his eyes giving no hint of emotion as he came forward to meet his opponent. Diana heard the cries of admiration and felt the tense excitement that surged through the throngs. These two were evenly matched, both in size and strength, as had been shown in earlier fights. They were now to test their skills against each other in the clash of life and death. One of them would fall, leaving the victor the celebrated champion of the day.

As Mario turned to face his opponent, he suddenly flung his sword from him and cried out, "Hear ye, Romans! I will not fight! I will die if I must, but I will not again fight to kill! I believe that Jesus Christ is the Son of God!"

Diana gasped and felt strength leave her body. Mario—a Christian? The other gladiator stopped and turned toward the Emperor, his expression never changing as he awaited the verdict. The Emperor did not hesitate.

"He is a Christian! Kill him!" Emperor Valerian roared above the swelling tide of anger in the gallery around him. "Do not spare his life!"

For an instant, sorrow flamed in the eyes of Mario's

opponent before he turned and advanced. Without flinching, Mario stepped forward to meet him. A moment later it was over. Mario had met his death, passing from life into eternity to meet his God.

The Christian who entered the arena next was slight in stature, but his face radiated confident hope. He knelt in the sand, making no effort to escape when the lion bounded toward him. In an instant his spirit had departed as well.

Diana stumbled from the gallery, rushing down the stairs and into the streets, where she collapsed to her knees. Covering her face with both hands, she cried out to any gods there were to show her where the justice was in life, and to take her away to join the loved ones who had departed.

Diana sensed a shadow as Athena stepped in front of her. "Are you all right?"

"Why couldn't Julian at least have set his slaves free?" Diana cried out. "Instead, he sold them to be killed!"

"Mario wasn't afraid to die. And neither was Rachel." Turning, Athena gazed up at the skies. "I've been reading the parchments Rachel gave me. They often speak of love, peace, and joy."

Diana's eyes widened. "She gave them to you?"

"Yes," answered Athena simply. "And I've read them all several times. But now I want you to have them."

"Why?" Diana whispered.

Athena's gaze was steady. "You were her closest friend, Diana. I think she would've wanted you to have them."

Diana took the parchments gently, smoothing her hand over the rough pages. "Tell me honestly, my lady. What has this book done for you?"

Athena smiled. "It showed me the cross of Christ, Diana. It showed me the way to find forgiveness of sins and peace with God. And if you read it with an open heart, it'll show you as well. I will pray for you."

Diana glanced briefly toward the Colosseum, her face shadowing. Athena's glance followed, and she spoke softly. "We cannot change what goes on there. But we can change our response to it."

"I will begin reading Rachel's gift tonight," Diana sated with resolve.

PARDON'S PRICE

CHAPTER NINETEEN

Justin couldn't have said why he found himself heading down the street that night to shops he seldom visited. Perhaps his need to be alone drew him there, where no one was likely to follow. Whatever the reason, he did not turn from the road that led deeper into the downtown streets of the city.

His steps halted before a pottery shop. He enjoyed pottery, but he didn't particularly feel like shopping tonight.

Just as he passed the shop, a voice called from behind him. "Justin!"

He glanced back. A young man with curly, dark hair stood in the doorway of the pottery shop. "Justin Gallus," he called again, his pleasant smile reaching his eyes. "Will you come back?"

Slowly, unwillingly, Justin turned and walked toward him. "Who are you?" he asked without preamble as he drew near.

"I am Philip Lucius. And you are Julian Gallus's nephew, yes? I have a message for you." Philip smiled and waved one hand. "Come in!"

How did this young man know his uncle? The question prompted Justin forward. Philip closed the door behind him and walked toward his desk. "I spoke with your cousin Rachel several times before she was sent to the arena," he said. "I hold her in the highest regards."

Justin swallowed hard. "She was special to me."

Philip's gaze was keen. "She told me that she talked with you about her faith."

"Yes, several times," Justin admitted. "I even visited Rachel in prison. I asked her about her faith—I thought I wanted what she had. But then she was killed in the arena." He paused, and Philip looked at him with sympathy. "And Mario, a slave from the Gallus villa, was killed today as well. But he seems to have become a Christian just before he died. I suppose he decided that proclaiming himself a Christian was the easiest way to end his life."

"It was more than that," answered Philip quietly. "He saw that the cross of Christ is the only way to eternal life. We will all understand the cross someday, either here or on judgment day. The Scriptures say that on that day, every knee will bow and every tongue confess that Jesus Christ is Lord."

"What was the message you had for me?" Justin asked after a long moment of silence.

"It's a letter, actually." Reaching into his desk, Philip lifted out a small white package and handed it to him.

As his eyes fell on the writing, Justin gasped. "To my

dear cousin Justin," he whispered, tracing the familiar handwriting with one finger. Overcome, he leaned against the desk and began to weep.

———◆———

Julian Gallus stood at his library window, gazing with unseeing eyes into the peristyle below. The stillness of the villa was so heavy it could be felt, and he could not escape its haunting echoes. The images of his beloved family and the part he had played in their deaths burned in his memory day and night.

He turned slowly, his hands grasping at the dagger that lay on his desk. His breath caught. Suicide was the only way out of this nightmare—but he simply could not do it. "There is life after death," his daughter had told him many years ago. Somehow this knowledge kept him from doing what he so desperately desired to do.

A knock sounded on the door, opening almost at once. "You sent for me, sir?" Justin rushed into the room, halting abruptly as his eyes fell on the dagger in the senator's hands.

"Yes, Justin, I did." Julian placed the dagger back on his desk and seated himself. "Sit down."

Justin's glance returned to the dagger before he took the chair directly before the high desk. "Yes, sir."

"I've been hearing a few things about you lately, Justin. I have called you in to ask if what I hear is true."

Justin met his gaze squarely. "Yes, sir, it is true. I have chosen to become a Christian, and I'm resigning from the army."

Julian's expression did not change. "You don't know

what this means."

"On the contrary," said Justin, leaning forward, "I know well what it means. I will be killed for my faith."

"Yes, you will face death." The senator's voice rang with steel. "The Emperor is most displeased with you, Justin, and I must warn you that there will be no mercy."

Justin spoke softly, his manner controlled and confident. "Jesus commands me to take up my cross and follow Him. I have purposed in my heart to do that."

"Then I have nothing more to say to you. You are dismissed."

"One word before I go." Justin rose slowly, his gaze steady on Julian's face. "I have something to tell you."

———————◆———————

"And how did he respond when you told him she was alive, sir?" Diana stood in the kitchen, kneading bread dough.

"For a long moment he simply sat there, motionless, and stared at me. I was beginning to think he didn't comprehend what I was saying." Justin paused and shook his head slowly. "When at last he did move, I was stunned to see tears in his eyes."

"Tears?" Diana stared at him.

"Even a hard heart can soften, Diana, and I believe that's what is happening with my uncle. Perhaps it's because his whole family was taken away from him, and because of the part he played in their deaths." He paused. "No, it's more than that. God is working in his heart."

Diana gazed at him. "Have you become a Christian too, sir?"

"I have," answered Justin assuredly.

Diana smiled. "So have I," she said quietly. "Please tell me, sir—what influenced you to make the decision?"

Justin's head came up. "Forget the 'sir,' Diana. I am not your master, and you are no longer a slave in my eyes."

"Yes, sir—I mean, Justin—sir." They laughed together.

"Well, I will tell you." Justin leaned back in his chair. "I visited with Philip Lucius a few days ago. He stayed up most of the night with me, explaining the faith until I believed." He looked at her. "Will you tell me your story, Diana?"

"Certainly, I will," Diana said. "Mario's testimony in the arena touched my heart profoundly. And when Athena gave me Rachel's pages of the Scriptures after she met me in the streets, I read until very late. Then I told God I will submit to His will and let Him be in charge of my life." She paused. "I am at peace now."

Justin nodded. "It's a peace that passes all understanding." He took a deep breath and said quietly, "I am leaving for the catacombs; it is the only place where I can dwell in safety. And, Diana—I think you should come too."

She started. "Sir?"

"You shouldn't stay here," he said firmly. "There's too much danger."

Diana held up one hand. "I know there's danger. But I feel I have a duty here. I don't think it's time for me to go yet."

Justin remained silent for a long moment. "I can't tell you to go against God's will," he said at length. "But I'll pray every day for you. If the senator discovers that you are a Christian—"

"I'm in God's hands," she reminded him softly.

He smiled then, his features relaxing. "As we all are."

"Will you not attempt to visit Rachel?" she asked as he pushed back his chair.

"That's where I am headed tonight," he answered. "I will take the risk of capture. I must see how she's doing and tell her of my faith. Do you have a message you wish for me to deliver to her?"

CHAPTER TWENTY

March 18, 259
" 'My soul is blessed by the Lord; it is lifted above my enemies on wings like eagles.' This is part of a song I'm writing—it's coming straight from my heart this afternoon!"

Rachel sat on a bench outside the Lucan villa where the sun could warm her face. It was the first day the weather had been warm enough to sit outside, and Rachel reveled in the fresh spring air. She felt so much better than she had two months ago. She recalled the pain she had felt after her surgery and the sense of doom when she realized she would never walk again. It had been too much to bear to think of the fact that she would always have to rely on others to meet her every need. Even so, God's grace had been present, giving her a will to live and gradually helping her to return to joy.

Rachel enjoyed writing. She enjoyed writing in her journal, a gift from the Lucan family on her seventeenth birthday. Smiling, she put down her stylus and recalled what Amata had just revealed to her: Philip Lucius was her brother-in-law!

Sitting beside each other on the bench, she and Amata had talked about their families. She, Adelpho, and their older sister Candace had grown up in this village, and Candace had married her childhood playmate, who turned out to be Philip. A year later, Candace died, leaving behind an infant daughter and a grieving, brand-new father. Philip left little Aquilina with Amata's parents and disappeared on a business trip. He told them later that the trip was an attempt to drown his grief with work.

Amata's family wished to keep Aquilina but felt that they were too poor. They had to let someone else take care of her. Amata was broken-hearted to think of losing her tiny niece, and one day she took to the hills, wanting only to be alone with her grief.

When Amata came to that part of the story, Rachel recalled a scene from her past. The girl she had met near the lake so long ago—could it be?

It was. She and Amata had met that day. With loud exclamations, they reveled in their reunion after five years. As Rachel told her story of the discovery of who her grandparents were, tears filled Amata's eyes. "To think that afternoon was the beginning of all that has brought you here!" she said. "I've never forgotten you, Rachel. And I'm so glad that we have met again."

She went on to say that the evening after she had run to the hills, Philip showed up again and told the family that he had found a place for his daughter. That's when Aquilina had been placed into Simon and Adara Severus's home. Through frequent contact with Simon and Adara, Philip had become a Christian.

Rachel picked up her stylus again and dipped it into the ink.

"Just thinking about Philip makes me wonder what's happening to all my loved ones—my grandparents, Diana, Justin, Mario. Will I ever see them again?"

Rachel shivered. Had the day gotten colder, or was it just a chill wind that had blown over her heart? She looked down at the song she'd started to write and thought about how to finish it. No words came.

———————◆———————

"Rachel? His Majesty and Lady Aemilia wish to see you," Adelpho announced playfully.

Rachel glanced up from her needlework and smiled. "The doctor and the queen of his heart, you mean?"

The physician was laughing as he came through the doorway. "Yes, it is as you say," he said.

Adelpho grinned and turned to leave. "Amata will be coming in soon with refreshments," he called over his shoulder.

"Thank you, Adelpho," Rachel said. "Hello, Dr. Marcus, Lady Aemilia. It's good to see you again."

"And you, Rachel," answered Aemilia, grasping her hand. "You are looking well these days."

"I feel well." Rachel let out a deep breath. "Through my

doctor and the whole Lucan family, God has worked healing in me. Even though I know I will never walk again, I trust that God has a purpose for my life."

"Of that I have no doubt." Aemilia squeezed her hand gently and smiled up at Dr. Marcus. "Tell her, Marcus."

Rachel looked quizzically from one to the other. "What is it?"

"Aemilia and I are getting married," Dr. Marcus told her, "and we would like for you to sing on our wedding day."

Rachel caught her breath. "You really want me to sing at your wedding?"

"Marcus told me how you love to sing, and we want a soloist," answered Aemilia. "You are free to write the song as you choose. We're planning to get married in May."

Rachel was speechless for a moment. Then she said firmly, "Well, then, if I am to write a song, I should be sitting out among the rosebuds for inspiration. Will you help me, Dr. Marcus?"

The bench against the villa's wall was framed with greening vines holding the hints of rosebuds swelling in the early spring sunshine. Rachel sighed with pleasure as she adjusted the scroll on her lap. Across the lawn, the doctor and Aemilia moved slowly toward the woods, talking companionably.

"We will walk this path together, hand in hand forever," Rachel wrote. Suddenly she stopped, sober thoughts welling up within her. Marriage. Such a beautiful unity that God Himself had created, this blending of two lives into one. But it was out of the question for her. She could never meet the expectations of a wife and mother without the use of her legs.

But dreams she had thought were lying on the altar before God stirred to life once more, reminding Rachel of the time when she had been well and whole, free to live a normal life. As she watched the young couple strolling into the sunset together, the battle within her became fierce, leaving her wrestling bitterly with her lot in life.

Pushing the unfinished song away, she reached for the Scriptures the physician had lent her, restlessly seeking hope and comfort in the inspired words.

Later that evening she wrote in her journal.

> God showed me that I am not alone and never will be, for I am His bride. His love for me is so vast that He died for my sins and paid the price of the pardon I enjoy today. Whatever God has for my future, I am committed to following Him the whole way.
>
> And I can't let myself believe that it will be marriage.

The girl in the glass that morning looked better than Rachel could remember seeing her in a long time. No longer pale with intense pain, her clear eyes revealed quiet peace within.

After she was taken outside to sit on the bench against the wall, Rachel sighed with pleasure and said to herself, "Why do I feel that something wonderful is about to happen? Is it just the wind bringing the fresh scent of spring, or the gorgeous colors of the sunrise?"

"Rachel!" The call broke into her reverie, vibrant in the clear morning air. Rachel's hand on her parchments froze.

"Rachel!" The call came again, and this time Rachel recognized the voice.

"Justin!" she cried, leaning forward. "Over here!"

The meeting was joyous, sparkling with laughter and tears. "Oh, it's so wonderful to see you again, Justin." Rachel's voice caught as she gripped her cousin's hand in hers. "I was just reminiscing about home yesterday, wondering what is happening with everyone. And now—this is like a gift straight from heaven!"

"I received your message a few days ago, and I came as quickly as I could," explained Justin, smiling broadly. "I asked Philip to come with me. He's in with his in-laws now to give us some time together first. I could hardly walk those last few miles fast enough! You're looking very well, I must say that."

Rachel's eyes sparkled as she leaned back against her pillows. "I feel better now than I have since . . ." She paused. "Since the day I went to the arena," she finished quietly.

Justin's eyes clouded. "Much has changed since then, Rachel. Your grandmother . . ." He paused.

"Tell me, Justin." Rachel's heart began to pound faster.

"She passed away soon after you went to the arena," Justin said softly, his eyes filled with compassion. "Another heart spell. But before she died, she became a Christian, according to Diana." He paused and then drew a parchment from his garments. "Diana sent a message along for you, Rachel."

Unable to speak, Rachel's hands trembled as she opened the letter and began to read.

Dear Rachel,

How I long to see you again. So much has happened within the last months that it seems impossible that our lives were at one time merely meaningless existence. It's plain to see that our lives are now governed by God's mighty hand.

While your grandmother was on her deathbed, she asked me to tell her everything I knew about your faith. She died a believer, Rachel—of this there is no doubt in my mind.

Diana went on to tell of what had happened to Mario and of how she became a Christian after seeing him die. She had wanted to come with Justin on this journey but felt that she needed to stay with the senator, whose mind was not well.

Keep me in your prayers, Rachel. The future appears dark, but I am trying to trust God. In His presence, there is only light.

As ever,
Diana

When Rachel finished reading, she had only one question. "Does my grandfather know that I'm still alive?"

Justin nodded and met her eyes. "He was moved to tears."

"Tears?" Rachel stared at him.

"It's as I told Diana." Justin leaned forward slightly. "God can work in even the hardest heart. I don't know how soft the senator's heart is yet, but I know God is working."

"The hardest heart," Rachel murmured. "Justin, has

God been working in your heart?"

"Indeed He has." Justin laughed softly. "I have joined the kingdom of Christ as well. In fact, I am going to the catacombs from here. It's too dangerous to remain in Rome after resigning from the army."

"Oh, Justin," Rachel cried. "My heart feels overwhelmed. I felt that something wonderful was going to happen today, but I never once thought of seeing you and hearing that you've become a believer!"

"I only plan to be here one day, Rachel." Justin hesitated. "The senator warned me that there would be no mercy for me."

Rachel leaned forward. "Can you tell me anything more about my grandfather?"

"There isn't much to tell, other than that he was considering . . . suicide." Justin paused as Rachel's head jerked up. "But, Rachel, Diana is there. I truly believe God has kept her there for a purpose."

"But, Justin! To think of him considering suicide—it makes me feel frantic." Rachel sank against the back of the bench. "How can I be at peace now, knowing this?"

"You must let the situation rest in God's hands." Justin gazed at her earnestly. "There's nothing you can do for him, Rachel, but God knows what to do."

Rachel didn't answer for a long moment. Finally she said, "This is something I will pray about without ceasing from now on."

"And I will pray with you." Justin stood from the bench. "Philip wanted to see you too, Rachel. I'll go call him now, if you'd like."

As Justin left, Rachel scanned Diana's letter again and thought of her grandfather. Would God actually ask her to sit idly by and do nothing while her grandfather's soul suffered such torture?

"Your promise, Lord," she whispered. "My thoughts are not your thoughts—what does this mean for me right now? Please be with my grandfather. I lift him to your throne of grace. Show him your abundant love, mercy, and pardon."

Pardon's Price

CHAPTER TWENTY-ONE

I'm glad to see you here, Rachel," said Philip, slipping down beside her on the bench.

It was strange how, in one heartbeat, her thoughts could change from a dreamy haziness to such clear vibrancy. Rachel straightened, hoping that Philip wouldn't see the sudden blush in her cheek. "I love to sit here, just to be alone with God and the nature around me," she said, turning to face Philip. "Somehow I always feel closer to God here than any other place."

"I can see why you like to come here." Philip crossed his arms behind his head as he leaned back. "It's a perfect view."

Rachel laughed softly. "If I could, I'd be out roaming the forests and meadows."

Philip's gaze on her face was searching. "You have suffered much."

Her eyes shadowed for a moment. "I still struggle at

times with the thought of never being able to walk again. I've always chafed at inactivity. But when I first woke up after going to the arena, I had to find myself again. It wasn't easy. That sort of trauma changes a person. But I am discovering again that life is beautiful, hard as it may be at times. Even though I can never walk again, I find that I can sit in heavenly places with Christ."

"Rachel, I wish you would share your story with my family," Philip said quietly. "I think it would influence them for Christ."

Rachel smiled. "I've already shared my story with Amata, and Aelius and Lydia have asked Justin and me to talk with them during the evening meal tonight. Adelpho is especially interested in Justin."

"I've noticed that." Philip's expression was pensive. "I hope Justin can help Adelpho to see that there is absolutely nothing in the army that is truly attractive. But my brother-in-law has a mind of his own when it comes to things like this."

"We can pray," Rachel said softly.

"Indeed." Philip smiled and turned to face her. "Rachel, you amaze me."

Rachel tilted her head quizzically.

"You've been through so much," Philip went on. "You have every right to feel bitter toward your grandfather, yet you aren't. You are living proof of a vessel God counts worthy to honor. Somehow, I believe that your story isn't going to stay here only among those who know you best. It will spread."

"What makes you so sure of that?"

"The fact that you can't walk will make those who come in contact with you stop and think. When they see your joy and acceptance of your handicap, they will wonder about it."

Rachel was silent for a moment. "You have an incredible story as well, Philip. Your wife died, leaving you behind with a daughter to bring up. And now you stay aboveground and face daily danger rather than seeking shelter in the catacombs."

"It's true that I face danger and that I've had some hardships in my life. But you're going to have more opportunities to share your story and bring glory to God because of your visible handicap."

Rachel nodded slowly. "I see what you mean. But why would God choose to make my life a testimony in this way? If I had the choice, I would walk to share it. Couldn't that be just as effective?"

"The ways of God are past finding out," Philip said quietly. "There's no way to tell just how effective your life story will be, but I believe there are exciting things in store for you."

Philip paused for a moment. Then, with conviction in his voice, he stated, "Rachel, I would like to be part of your story. Would you consider giving me your hand in marriage?"

———————

That night, Rachel pulled out her journal, her heart overflowing with emotion. She knew she had to write.

The Lucan family was touched when Justin and I shared our testimonies tonight. I know they are considering the Way, and that brings me great joy. I'm glad I was able to concentrate on talking about what God has done for me, because I wasn't sure I could think about anything else after my afternoon with Philip. Nobody else knows about his proposal yet; I needed time to think about it.

Does Philip realize what he's asking? I don't want to cripple his life! He tried to convince me that love would see us through the hardest times, but I still find myself holding back. I can hardly believe that he actually loves me enough to see past my handicap and view me as a woman.

And dear little Aquilina—I love her, but can I be a mother to her with no legs?

Oh, God, I am desperate for your wisdom tonight! I don't want to make Philip a miserable man. Help me not to make a mistake in this decision.

"I will sing of the mercies of the Lord forever: with my mouth will I make known thy faithfulness . . ."

Diana stopped reading as the sound of a horse's hooves reached her ears. Seldom did they get visitors these days— a vast contrast to what it had been like before the mistress's death.

The elderly man on the cot beside her did not open his eyes as Diana stood up. Indeed, he seemed totally unaware that she was even near. Diana stifled a sigh and slowly laid aside the parchments that used to belong to Rachel, carrying them with her as she left the room. This past week, the senator had been lying in bed every day with his eyes closed and his body stiff and still as though in a trance. His crying out at night had become more frequent, and by day he sent for her often and required her to sit by his side.

With so much time on her hands, Diana had begun reading the Scriptures aloud—hesitantly at first, then more bravely as he made no objection. Though she had no assurance that he ever listened, he usually did seem to relax as she read.

Now as she walked slowly down the hall to receive the visitor, Diana wondered why she was still here. She wanted nothing more than to leave—to go and see Rachel again, to move ahead with her life. Why, then, did she feel so strongly about staying?

She was surprised to find Philip Lucius in the atrium. "Hello, Diana," he greeted her. "I've come to tell you that Rachel wants to visit her grandfather," he went on, his eyes clouding with concern. "And she wants to do it as quickly as possible."

Diana stared. "Well, I'd love to see her again—but there's so much danger. Think of what happened the last time she came back!"

"She has thought of that," Philip assured. "But she says that she can't feel at peace until she does all she can to make things right between the two of them." He shook his head. "The knowledge that he was considering suicide haunts her unceasingly. She's determined to come before it's too late."

Diana was silent for a moment. "It's useless to try to change Rachel's mind when it's made up," she said at length. "But I truly don't think it'll do any good. Julian's heart is still too hard to let Christ enter."

"We must have faith, Diana," Philip said softly. "I don't believe God would impress this upon Rachel's heart without a purpose."

Diana nodded slowly. "When should I expect her arrival?"

"In a couple of days, at the most."

"Very well. I'll be waiting."

As Diana returned to the senator's chamber, she admitted to herself what she hadn't dared to tell Philip. *Julian is hovering on the brink of insanity—I'm sure of it. Can Rachel handle that?*

———

Rachel never told Diana everything that transpired the day she was carried into the room where her grandfather lay and was left alone with him. She only mentioned enough to let Diana know that all was clear between them at last.

Within two hours of Rachel's arrival, Julian Gallus passed away, leaving earth for eternity. Rachel and Diana were the only ones with him when he died, Rachel having summoned Diana when she saw his breathing becoming more labored. "I don't know if he became a Christian or not," Rachel said. "But he's in the hands of God now."

Diana gazed at the slim hand holding the large, weathered one. "You truly did love him, didn't you?" she asked softly.

Rachel's eyes shimmered with tears. "Yes, I did. Diana, if he is in eternity without God . . ." She shuddered and took a deep breath. "Oh, if there were only a way to be sure."

"You have done all you can," answered Diana thoughtfully.

Rachel nodded. "Philip told me the same thing." She

shook her head. "But I need more faith," she said softly, as though to herself.

"Will you be here for the burial?" Diana's tone was hushed.

Rachel shook her head slowly. "I want to attend, but there's too much danger for that. I will say goodbye here."

Diana nodded and left the room silently, closing the door behind her. There was no need for her to stay at the estate now. She would leave with Philip and Rachel in the morning.

Why had she chosen to remain here for the final days of the senator's life? She felt troubled as she trudged up the stairs to her chamber. She doubted that she had done any good.

In her room, her eyes fell on the parchments containing the holy words she had read to herself and to the senator. Why did I read to him when it didn't seem to do any good? she wondered. Because a gentle whisper within had prompted her to do so, she reminded herself. "Perhaps I chose to remain behind so that Julian could have another chance to be received into your kingdom," she whispered to God. "You alone know whether or not the senator is with you for eternity, because you are the judge of his soul. But I know I have done what I can, and I know I can trust you with the rest."

PARDON'S PRICE

CHAPTER TWENTY-TWO

Rachel gazed out the window at the twilight vista. Her heart, though weighted with sadness, was at peace. She knew she could rest in the knowledge that her grandfather was indeed in God's hands, and she had done what she could.

In the distance she could hear the bleat of goats as they bounded down the mountain. As the evening's charm and beauty filled her soul, Rachel caught a glimpse of Philip walking to the barn with Adelpho. She smiled. *Two good men,* she thought. Adelpho was one person who had been touched by God's love since she'd come to live with the Lucan family. Before Justin had left for the catacombs, he told Rachel that Adelpho had come to him the night after they had told the family their testimonies. Justin and Adelpho had talked until Adelpho gave up his dream to join the Roman army and decided to join the heavenly army instead. The thought filled Rachel with joy.

Philip looked her way now, his eyes glinting as he smiled broadly and waved. Rachel's heart thrilled as she waved back. She had spoken with the physician about Philip's proposal, asking him if it would be wise to accept. Dr. Marcus had told her that he could see nothing wrong with accepting Philip's request. If anyone could handle such a marriage, it would be Philip. He had been through much already, and he was a mature Christian.

"Rachel? Is it all right if I come in—or would you rather just sit there and watch the love of your heart?" Diana's teasing voice broke into her reverie.

Rachel grinned and spoke without turning her head. "What do you think?"

"I think it goes without saying." Diana laughed and joined her at the window.

"You'll feel the same way someday, Diana," Rachel said with conviction.

Diana's face sobered. "I don't know about that."

Something in her tone caused Rachel to glance up sharply. "Let me guess," she said without preamble. "When Justin left for the catacombs, a part of your heart went with him."

A sudden flush colored Diana's cheek, giving her away. "How did you—"

"I can read you like a book, Diana," laughed Rachel. "I've had years of practice, you know."

Diana shrugged. "How I feel about it doesn't matter, Rachel. Nothing will ever come of it. For so many years, Justin thought of me as a mere slave."

"Don't be so sure about that." Rachel leaned forward. "I know he thought a lot of you." She paused and then added, "When we go down to the catacombs, you will see him again. Perhaps you'll discover your answer—" She stopped as Diana shook her head slightly.

"So you've decided to hold your wedding ceremony in the catacombs?" Diana asked calmly, changing the subject.

Rachel smiled, her gaze returning to the window. "Indeed we have. I only stayed here these last few months because it was dangerous to be moved during recovery from operation. But now that I've endured the trip to Rome and back, we are leaving for the catacombs as soon as we're able to." After a pause, she added quietly, "My heart is so filled with the goodness of God that I feel I could sing all day and all night."

Amata walked into the room in time to hear the last of Rachel's words. "Are you planning to sing at your wedding?" she inquired.

"Actually, yes," Rachel said with a laugh. "Philip wanted me to, and when we decided to hold a double wedding with Dr. Marcus and Aemilia, it worked out perfectly."

"You're holding a double wedding?" Amata exclaimed.

"Yes, we just decided that. And Philip has decided to sell his pottery shop in Rome. We're planning to make our home in the catacombs. Diana will come too, at least for now." Glancing ruefully at the blanket covering her lap, she said, "It's difficult to accept that I won't be able to fulfill all the needs of housework myself, but I trust that God will help me do what I can. And," she added, smiling, "Philip has talked of making a one-person wagon for me so I can wheel myself around. Have you ever heard of such a thing?"

"Well, it sounds as though you have it all worked out," Amata smiled. "I'm sure Adara is glad that you'll be near her. After all these years, Aquilina is like her own daughter."

Rachel nodded. "I wouldn't want to take them too far away from each other. Philip feels the same way."

Diana glanced up from the scroll where Rachel had written several lines of song lyrics. "Have you been practicing your songs?"

Before Rachel could answer, Amata said, "I've certainly heard her singing a lot the last few days! I never get tired of it. I think she should start singing in the village streets so that more people could hear her."

"You have more ambitious dreams than I do," Rachel laughed softly. "But it is an enticing thought. I would love to sing for people the rest of my life—point the way to God, lift their spirits, and sing words that comfort the soul."

"Well, even if you never get to sing for the villagers, I'm sure your fellow Christians in the catacombs will be blessed by your music," Diana assured her.

Silver notes of laughter broke into the sweet symphony falling on Philip's ears. Rachel smiled and began to sing faster, accommodating the small girl whirling about the chamber. Pausing, she leaned forward and called, "Is that enough for now, Aquilina?"

Aquilina turned, her face wreathed in smiles. "No!" she shouted. "Sing more, Rachel!"

Philip laughed and swung her up into his arms. "In a few hours, Aquilina, you will call Rachel 'Mama'!"

Rachel exchanged a special smile with Philip and glanced down at the scroll on her lap. "My soul is blessed by the Lord; it is lifted above my enemies on wings like eagles," she lifted up her voice once more. "My desire is to fly to my Lord." She paused for a moment before letting her voice soar with the final lines. "While I am on earth, I will enter heavenly places when I praise the Lord. From glory to glory I will fly until I enter eternity!"

———————

The rich tones of a hymn sung with heartfelt meaning echoed through the vaulted chamber lit with the flickering flames of torches. Rachel felt a hush steal over her heart. "Are you ready to go in?" Philip was asking her.

"I am, indeed," she answered radiantly.

Philip and Adelpho carried Rachel's cot to the front of the chamber, where many Christians were assembled for the special day that would unite two couples in marriage.

Rachel sang a song about the heavenly Bridegroom and His bride. "He longs for her, He waits for her, He woos her with tender affection . . ." As she sang, Rachel's soul felt suspended between the past and the future. Behind her lay the path filled with pain, questions, and pardon given and received. Before her lay the promise of beauty for ashes.

As the ceremony continued, Rachel bowed her head and prayed silently, *Oh, Lord, may my life to be a glorious symphony for you. I want to be a vessel that you can sanctify and use to the fullest as you live in me. Thank you for giving my life meaning.*

PARDON'S PRICE

Epilogue—Ten Years Later

March, 269

Dear Rachel,

Greetings in the precious name of our risen Lord and Savior, Jesus Christ.

Do you realize how much you are loved, Rachel? During our visits to the villages outside Rome, many people mention you. Your story is widely known, and your testimony is beautiful. It breathes in the songs you write and sing, and it lifts the spirits of those who hear. You are a source of joy and cheer, and I believe you are able to touch more people with your handicap than you'd be able to otherwise.

With our family living in Rome, our visits don't happen very often. That's why I was so glad that Justin was asked to preach at the baptism in your village. I knew at once that this was one trip my husband couldn't take without the rest of his family. I am eager to see you!

And Aquilina is nearly fifteen years old. It's amazing how the years go by! I'm sure my daughter

Rachel will be eager to learn to know her. Rachel is only nine, but she looks up to older girls and gets along well with them. Watching her, I sometimes find myself transported back to the days when we were young girls, and I relive the events that shaped our lives. Isn't it such a blessing to know that God sees the whole picture and works out everything for good?

We have had relative peace and rest from persecution for a number of years, though several accounts regarding faithful martyrs still drift back to us. But if persecution ever comes to us again, we can face it with peace instead of fear; for what we suffer at the cross of Christ is not worthy to be compared with what awaits us after death.

It is in this promise that we find true rest.

Peace be with you, Rachel.

Diana

"Beloved, think it not strange concerning the fiery trial which is to try you, as though some strange thing happened unto you: But rejoice, inasmuch as ye are partakers of Christ's sufferings; that, when his glory shall be revealed, ye may be glad also with exceeding joy." 1 Peter 4:12-13

PARDON'S PRICE

ABOUT THE AUTHOR

Diane Yoder hones her story-writing craft in southern Indiana, where she lives with her parents and four of her siblings. She has enjoyed writing as long as she can remember. Her first story was published when she was fourteen years old. Through the encouragement of her friends and family, she has been inspired to keep pursuing her dream of more publications. This is her first book.

Diane is a member of Living Waters Mennonite Church. She delights in the beauty she finds in nature, music, words, and people. Her desire and prayer is that her readers will learn to trust the Savior and receive His love.